DEAD AIR

ACADEMY'S RISE
BOOK THREE

LIA DAVIS

LAINIE ANDERSON

Dead Air

Published by Davis Raynes Publishing

PO Box 224

Middleburg, FL 32050

DavisRaynesPublishing.com

Cover by Glowing Moon Designs

Formatting by Glowing Moon Designs

The Academy's Rise Trilogy is dedicated to our amazing support team. Tricia, Jenee, Renee, Mary, Tory: You're amazing. We don't know what we would've done without you. This series certainly wouldn't have been as good without you. All our love.

Dead Air

Academy's Rise, book 3

A Collective World Novel

Our biggest fight is yet to come.

I watched my sisters claim their fated mates with my heart full for their happiness.

Now it's time to face my own mates. Two of them have been at my side, and I'm waiting for my third. After all, it's now a family tradition to have three mates. I wonder if reality can be as good as the fictional worlds I love to live in.

Our world isn't all rainbows and hellhound puppies. There's something coming bigger than any of us have ever faced.

Now that I've tapped into my massive powers, I will do what it takes to save my family and my mates. I've had just about enough running and hiding behind wards and our sentries. It's time to end the threat from Hell once and for all.

Enough is enough.

CHAPTER ONE

"Stop fidgeting," Meda whispered as I adjusted the folds of my flowing black skirt again. It wasn't wrinkled, but I was uncomfortable in it. The last thing I wanted to do was to say goodbye to one of my sentries, and waiting for his family to come to the pyre was torture.

My heart shattered when I heard Elijah had died. He'd given his life to save my mom's—his High Alpha. It was his job, his calling, and he hadn't hesitated.

But being grateful didn't make saying our final goodbye any easier. I picked at my skirt again, the feel of the thick wool itchy against my skin. I should've worn tights. Taking in a shaking breath, I pulled at the waistband.

Harper pressed her shoulder into mine and linked our fingers, pulling my hand away from my clothes. What would I have done without her and Noah? My heart felt like a gaping wound as it was.

Once Meda found her mates, it opened my attraction and friendship with Harper to a whole new level. We were fated mates. And we were more than okay with that. Chances were, we would've ended up dating anyway.

The big surprise was Noah. I'd never pinpointed my sexuality before, but I'd leaned toward being attracted to women. Not that I was repulsed by men, but they weren't generally the subject of my fantasies.

As my sentry, Noah had always been there and had been a close friend and confidant. After all, if you couldn't trust your sentries, then who could you trust?

The desires that opened up when the mating urge slammed into us made our already strong friendship even stronger. There was no denying it, so why fight it? We'd kept it quieter than Meda and Tala, choosing to slip our new dynamic into our everyday life. It had been accepted without a lot of hoopla, which I appreciated. I wasn't a fan of fuss and attention.

When Tala found *her* three mates after Meda's three, it was apparent that I was destined to find three as well. It seemed we had a pattern going. Each of my sisters mated a vampire, a lycan, and a witch. I had my vampire and my lycan, so I expected a witch to fall into my lap any day. Adding someone new to the dynamic wasn't going to be easy.

Releasing a sigh, I scanned the cemetery at the edge of the Collective Estate property. We didn't use it often. Lycans generally preferred cremation, and vampires almost exclusively preferred it. Their bodies tended to disintegrate— depending on their age—anyway. I wondered what my body would do when I died.

A chill breeze caressed my cheek, my element saying hello. I closed my eyes and lifted my head to commune with the air. Winter wasn't far off. I could sense it in my element. To me, the air carried voices and scents, sometimes feelings.

We stood at Elijah's funeral pyre, waiting for my mom and the *niswi*, all three of my fathers, to arrive with Elijah's family. Mom would give a speech as would each of my dads.

My nose tingled as thoughts of Elijah formed, and his ever-smiling face entered my mind. Noah wrapped an arm around my waist, pulling me into him. I thankfully rested my head on his chest and fought back the tears. Elijah wouldn't have wanted us to cry for him.

Ami, you okay?

I smiled at Meda's telepathic question. *Yeah, I'll be fine.*

Glancing over at Tala, I expected her to be looking for a way to escape the funeral without being rude. But she seemed to have her emotions in check. I sensed her shields were up to block out her empathy, which was understandable. Poking at her emotions, I realized she was calm. The presence of her mates made a big difference for her.

Meda stood at the front of the group with her mates, waiting for Mom and the *niswi*. In their absence, she was the leader of the Collective. We all were, and we all had to act like it. Even our mates. Surprise for them. Goodbye regular life. Hello leadership.

Elijah's family moved into sight down the long path from the Collective government house to the pyre, where we stood with the growing crowd of vampires, Lycans, and several witch families. I met Elijah's mom's gaze, our excellent eyesight giving us the ability to see each other down the path, and my vision blurred with tears.

The pain on her face was palpable. She had other sons, but Elijah had been her oldest. I'd attended many family dinners at his house, especially as a child. If my parents had to go out of town, there were only a few homes they'd allow my sisters and me to stay at. The Bradburn house was always my favorite. Elijah's mom was a reader and book collector. She always had something new for me to read. When I got older I learned she'd written many of the books I'd read and loved over the years.

I held her gaze, sharing her suffering and silently supporting her.

That was when I scented him. Gasping, I snapped my gaze to the witch following Elijah's parents and younger brothers. My third mate. His dark brown hair was cut above his ears, neatly styled, and his chocolate eyes held my stare. There was confusion in his depths at first, then a twitch of his lips told me he knew who I was, besides being one of the hybrid triplets. He knew *what* I was.

My pulse kicked up a few beats per second. This was not the time to meet another mate. How could I feel the explosion of passion for someone while grieving for a friend? It was disrespectful to the family. It was disrespectful to my friend who had given his life for my mother.

I forced myself to tear my gaze from him. But it was hard. And he probably was too...

Stop it, Ami. I chastised myself for the inappropriate thoughts. *Now is not the time.* I'd deal with the hot witch later.

My mom was the last to approach the pyre, per lycan tradition. Elijah had been a vampire, but his parents wanted him honored in a new mixed ceremony, blending the lycan and vampire traditions into a beautiful service. It was the first we'd done this way.

My dad opened the service. He walked to the front of the pyre and stared at Elijah's body for several moments. I still couldn't bring myself to look up at it. My attention strayed over to Sarah Bradburn. Her gaze was glued to the body of her son, on the wooden table built to hold him.

Dad cleared his throat. "Thank you all for coming. I'm pretty sure everyone knows me, though I see a few witches I'm unfamiliar with. I am Kane, once King Heir to the vampires, now High King of the Collective. I usually love getting up in front of everybody and having a good long talk, as many of you know, but not today." Dad paused and took a deep breath. "Elijah Bradburn was one of the Collective's brightest young sentries. I've known his father,

Joe, since I was Elijah's age." I snuck a glance at Joe Bradburn, my Dad's friend as long as I could remember. Joe had invented the sunscreen all vampires wore today to be able to go into the sun any time they wanted.

"Joe and Sarah took care of my girls many times over the years. Then, when he was old enough, Elijah took on the role. A feat some would call impossible, wrangling my girls. But he managed it, and he did it well."

Dad stopped and put his fingers to his eyes. He'd been particularly fond of Elijah. "I'm sorry," he whispered before looking at the crowd. "Elijah saved my wife, without hesitation, without a second thought. Your High Alpha and our unborn baby are only here because of the bravery of Elijah Bradburn."

He held his right fist over his heart, a sign of honor for Lycans. It was no mistake that the vampire leader of the Collective was the one to do the lycan gesture for honor. This was part of the blending of the ceremonies. The Lycans in the crowd repeated the sign, then slowly, most of the vampires and witches did as well.

It was a good sign that everyone followed suit. The vampire and lycan merger hadn't been easy. All my life we'd dealt with small rebellions and prejudices between the two groups. Over time, it was getting better and would continue to improve.

My generation was largely without the anger and resentment of our parents. That helped the parents learn to open their minds and hearts. Sometimes.

After a solid minute, Dad moved his hand away from his heart and backed up, taking his place to my mom's right. My Paw stepped forward. "Hello." My heart ached for him. Elijah had been a favorite of his as well. Elijah had been everyone's favorite, really. "Elijah Bradburn was a vampire, and I'm a lycan, obviously. I'm Voss, by the way, for those that don't know me." He gave an awkward little wave before continuing. He'd always been a terrible public speaker, but he'd wanted to do this. "Before I started teaching at the academy, I was in charge of sentry training."

Paw had been obsessed with shifter history for as long as I could remember. Eventually, he'd moved on to vampire and witch history as well. It had made perfect sense for him to teach the class when the University opened. To do that, he'd had to give up his training duties.

"Elijah was a joy to train. He was passionate about the work and dedicated to learning and improving. And he had *such* a knack for it. When it came time to choose permanent sentries for our girls, he was a natural selection. We all agreed easily that he should be on their detail."

Paw's head went back. From my angle, I could only see his profile, but it was clear he was swallowing down tears. "I'd like to share a story about Elijah. I don't know if he ever realized I'd seen him do this, but it stuck with me. We were in the woods, in Elijah's pledge year. Every Collective member is eligible to apply and try out to be a sentry. We give each of them a fair chance to prove their ability. We also give plenty of time for them to improve. Not everyone that comes to us is born with the skills needed. Many of our best sentries got where they are through hard work and determination."

He laughed and shook his head. "Elijah, he was born with it. A natural. He's got..." He cut off and pressed his lips together before continuing. "He had more defensive ability in one arm than his poor dad ever dreamed of having."

Paw turned his head and gave Joe Bradburn a sad smile after saying it. Joe had started as only my Dad's friend, but the *niswi* were very close, and Joe had become friends with all of them. Joe didn't smile back, though, just stood stoically as tears streamed down his face. Poor Paw, his joke hadn't gone over well. Poor Joe.

"We were running an obstacle course through the woods, not far from here. Another sentry, one we weren't sure would make it through the pledge year, was having trouble. I'd snuck around to watch the kids go through the worst part of the course, the ropes." He chuckled ruefully. "We don't just make them swing on ropes, then balance and walk on them. We also grease the ropes."

The crowd gave a subdued laugh. Paw shrugged. "Gotta make sure they're strong. That day, we had a straggler. Elijah had already made it to the end, but when his friend didn't pop through right behind him, he went back. Now, you have to understand how competitive these kids get on this course. Especially vampires to vampires and Lycans to Lycans. Elijah wasn't immune to this competition, either. But when he finished—and finished first, I might add, he waited on all the pledges. There are a few dangerous spots in the course, and he didn't know it at the time, but we keep people posted near those spots to help if any real trouble breaks out."

Paw sucked in a deep breath. "I—" His voice broke. He cleared his throat and tried again. "I watched that boy go back and find his friend. He encouraged, and shouted, and coached until his friend finished the course. That straggler is now one of our best sentries."

The crowd clapped, and many of the Lycans put their fists over their hearts again. Paw did as well. "I agree. Elijah was full of honor. He was one of the best sentries we've ever seen. He was an even better man."

Paw bowed his head, and then bowed at the waist, facing Elijah's body on the pyre. I couldn't stop myself from peeking at the crowd to see who else was mimicking the movement.

Everyone did. The bow was a vampire concession of honor and dignity. Typically, it was reserved for royalty or visiting ambassadors of other lands or species, but even then, the visitor had to be pretty powerful to get the honorific. It was the highest honor bestowed by the vampires, to bow to another.

My heartbeat quickened as I watched the entire crowd bow for Elijah.

I turned my head down before anyone caught me doing it wrong. Elijah would've been beside me, looking at me and making funny faces while everyone else bowed.

Paw stayed bowed for a solid minute to mirror Dad's gesture, then he stood and backed into his place to the left of my mom. Papa wasn't speaking, but he would light the pyre while my mother spoke. He'd been close to Elijah as well, but didn't think he could do it.

Mom stepped forward. "I'm pretty sure you all know me." The crowd tittered, most with tears in their eyes. Everyone knew of the female High Alpha who had a harem of men as mates. She was the stuff of legends.

"The Collective would like to bestow our highest Medal of Honor onto Elijah Bradburn posthumously." She turned to her left, where Tala stood, holding a black jewelry box. "This medal has only been given a handful of times over the years, and only for acts of bravery on behalf of the High Alpha. Elijah will be commemorated in our government building with a plaque, and a painting of his handsome face will be hung in our Hall of Honor."

Mom turned to face the Bradburns, where they stood opposite my sisters and me. "In addition, the Bradburn children will be given scholarships for the University, should they choose that path in life." That had been my idea. I thought Sarah might appreciate her remaining children not becoming sentries. If the University was free to them, we hoped they'd opt to take that route.

Mom stepped forward and handed the Bradburns the medal. Joe remained frozen in place, his eyes on his son's body, but Sarah gave my mother a sad smile and mouthed, "Thank you."

Mom turned back to the pyre and nodded at Papa. "Elijah Bradburn, rise high in death. May your place among the ancestors be honored, and your joy shine upon us." She put her right fist over her heart, then bowed again for a solid minute, while the sounds of the flames filled the air. I funneled a little magic toward the fire and pushed the smoke up and away from the crowd.

The flames moved quickly, and I realized Meda was giving them a little push, having them engulf Elijah's body and remove the sight of their son's burning corpse from the view of his parents.

We stood at the fire until the pyre was completely engulfed, then my mother stepped back, a sign that the crowd could quietly disperse. Before anyone moved, a silky-smooth voice carried through the air. "What a shame."

We whirled, my *niswi* into defensive crouches. My mom gasped when she saw who stood behind us. As soon as our sentries saw the *niswi* move in front of Mom, they did the same to us.

A tall woman with long white-blonde hair stood

behind us, dabbing at her eyes. She wore a full-length black dress, fitted to her voluptuous form.

"Hello, Kane, Jillian." The blonde-haired beauty nodded in their direction. "Such a sad day. Elijah was a bright boy. It's always hard when they're taken young, isn't it?"

"Trinity," my Dad growled. "How in the hell are you here?"

"Haven't you heard? I had a funeral of my own to attend. You'll remember the death of my daughter? Calista."

CHAPTER TWO

ury quickly replaced my shock. It was
because of Calista that we had to say
our goodbyes to our friend. If Trinity thought she
was going to come in and get revenge on behalf of
her psycho daughter, she was gravely mistaken.

The *niswi* rushed into action, barking out orders
to the sentries. Mom turned, grabbing my brothers
and sisters and leaving Trinity to us. Mom and her
personal sentry and best friend, Angel, gathered the
kids into a protective circle that Meda's mate, Sterling, and his parents created for them without being
asked.

Meda and Tala stood on either side me, and our
sentries and mates took the front line as a sea of

demons rushed out from the surrounding forest. As a unit, we charged forward. Meda conjured a sword while calling her fire to cover it. I felt Tala draw on my air to freeze her water into long thick icicles to use as weapons. I called on Meda's fire to heat my air as I formed a mini-cyclone, then pushed it at the crowd of demons.

I had no idea how many from the funeral behind us joined in the fray. The demons hit us so fast it was impossible to tell what was happening more than a few feet around me.

A dark, but familiar presence touched my awareness, and I smiled. Phenex. Our non-sexual mate shifted into his hellhound form and attacked the demons, cutting through them like they were children at play.

Nice. Since we met Calista and dealt with her evil plots to kill us, I'd learned to embrace my darker side.

Ami. Meda's voice filled my mind.

Yep? I switched to making icicles, whipping them together quickly and sending them toward the demons at chest height. Some hit, some didn't.

Take my power. Tala and I are better fighters. Stay behind us and build up a big ball of energy and fire.

Oh, hell yes.

I fell back, hiding behind my sisters. Meda must've talked to the sentries, because I felt Harper at my back, ensuring nobody got to me from behind. She'd gotten two short-swords from somewhere, I saw them flashing out of the corner of my eye. One of the witches must've conjured them.

Centering myself, I ignored the din around me, completely trusting my sisters, mates and sentries to keep me safe. It took too long to do this, we had to get faster at it, practice it.

Slowly, I built up a mass of power: Meda's fire, Tala's water, and my air, and I fed energy into it. Pulling from the forest, my sisters, and our mates, I even tried to tap into our Hell power, but I couldn't get it to open to me. I had to work with the power available to me here at the moment.

Harper jostled against me, breaking my focus and my feed of energy. I held an enormous ball of power and fire in front of me. Using my wind, I lifted it, then stood on my tiptoes, looking for the best place to send it.

Trinity fought my *niswi* not six feet in front of me, dancing around and laughing. She was playing with them. Focusing on her and the demons around her, I elongated the ball, lifted it higher, and threw it.

The demons around Trinity evaporated, as did several rows of them behind her. She staggered back with a gasp, looking for the source of the power surge. I ducked before she saw me. How had that not killed her? Not many creatures in this world could survive a direct hit with that much energy and power. For what I knew of Trinity, she was a vampire. However, she was getting power from somewhere, or someone.

Meda.

Yeah, I saw. Meda's tone in my head was lethal. She was pissed or scared. With her, they were pretty much the same. Her fear made her angry. We didn't have time for all three of us to create another energy ball that big.

So we each create smaller ones and attack her with them, Tala added with a snarl.

That might work. I moved to stand between my sisters. Our sentries seemed to be in sync with us and able to read our body language well enough to know what we needed them to do. They positioned themselves around us to provide a protective barrier. Together, my sisters and I combined our powers as each of us formed a basketball-size energy ball, adding in our combined elements.

We threw our balls of power at Trinity. She stumbled back, so we did it again, and again. We made our balls larger every time we formed new ones. Trinity seemed to deflect them like they were nothing more than large gnats.

"Why the fuck is she not dying?" Tala growled out.

"Maybe this isn't our big battle." As soon as my words left my mouth dread slammed into me.

Meda used her fire to cover her whole body. I glanced at her to see that she glared at Trinity. "One more time."

Tala and I didn't argue. The three of us lifted our arms and instead of making three energy balls, we merged our efforts into making one large one, bigger than the one I made. We put everything we had into it. By the time I stopped pushing energy and air into the ball, it was twice the size of the one I'd made alone.

It wasn't until we threw it at Trinity that we realized she was ready and had thrown one of her own. The two balls slammed into each other. Meda screamed, "Down!"

We hit the ground and so did all the Collective who'd stayed to fight. The blast from the energy balls crashing into each other lit up the sky with bright white light. When the light dimmed, then disappeared, we looked around. Trinity was gone.

Where did she go?

Pushing to a stand, I called my element to listen to any secrets the air carried.

Nothing happened. Panic rose within me. I reached for Meda's fire and Tala's water. There was nothing. Focusing, I tried harder, pushing into my sisters' minds. Meda wasn't hot. Tala wasn't swimmy. And my air, my light, soul freeing air. It was gone. I gasped, sinking to my knees. "Trinity took our elements."

My words were barely a whisper but my mates and sisters heard them. I glanced at Meda for some kind of guidance. She patted her chest and stomach as if she'd find her fire hidden in a pocket.

Tala looked at me blankly, holding her hands out in front of her, twisting them around as if waiting for her water to rise. "What do we do?" she whispered as she looked back to her hands. "It feels so wrong."

Meda grabbed my hand and tugged me to Mom and the *niswi.* "We'll figure it out." When we reached Mom and our younger siblings, Meda picked up Griffin, our youngest brother, and cradled him to her. "Is everyone okay?"

Dad glared at each of us but his anger wasn't directed at us. He was pissed at Trinity. "Everyone back to the manor." He pointed to a few people standing nearby. "Coordinate everyone to get the wounded back. We can tend to them there. The schools and the Estate are going on lock down." Looking around the crowd, he pointed again. I didn't bother looking to see who he was assigning tasks to. "The elementary school is empty?"

"Yes, classes canceled for this." I didn't recognize the voice. It might've been the new principal.

"Good. Take a group of fighters to the college. Get everyone to the manor. And start the call chain. Anyone that wants protection, they're welcome to come." He looked around at the crowd, then raised his arm and waved it in a circle. "Make it happen," he shouted. "Now!"

My sisters and I followed our parents to the Estate. Tala walked beside Mom with their arms looped together. We'd lost this battle. Lost a few sentries in the fight. And lost our elements. How would we fight off a bigger battle? This wasn't it. This wasn't the end. Trinity was sure to return. How?

Harper grabbed one of my hands while Noah took the other. Feeling eyes on me, I glanced over my shoulder and saw the hot olive-skinned witch watching me as he walked behind us. With a frown, I met Harper's gaze. She leaned in and pressed a comforting kiss on my trembling lips then pulled me closer to her. Noah kept hanging on, a tight grip on my hand. I sighed and rested my head on her shoulder as we entered the Manor.

When we sat on the sofa, Phenex appeared. He squatted in front of me and cupped my cheek. "You okay?"

I covered his hand and nodded, tears slipping past my lashes and down my cheeks. "Our elements are gone."

"I know." Dropping his head to my knees, he shuddered. "I'm sorry."

Meda and Tala walked up behind him, and he stood, drawing my sisters into a hug, one on each side. He kissed each of their foreheads, and they sank into him. "This is only the beginning. We need to train harder than we have been."

We nodded. Meda's face hardened and Tala's nostrils flared.

Dad cleared his throat as he watched us from the center of the big room. Then he crossed to us with Paw, Papa, and Mom in tow. All our mates gathered around. We must have looked like a small army.

Meda and Tala stepped out of Phenex's embrace as Phenex nodded to Dad and Mom. "I'm going to pop down and see what kind of information I can get from the demon hordes."

When our parents nodded, Phenex dematerialized.

Meda straightened her spine and stared at our parents. "We've been keeping a secret. A big one." Sighing, she squared her shoulders and got on with it. "You should know, the big battle from Tala's vision is still coming. It may be bigger than we anticipated."

Mom growled and threw her arms in the air. "You should've told us immediately so we could prepare!"

Tala cut in. "We were waiting for the right time to tell you. Poppy said to let you rest for a day, just be with you and family. Then we had to deal with the funeral and school, we didn't have time."

Meda took a breath, and I guessed it was to calm her growing irritation. "You were recovering from the fight at the hotel-mansion. We were going to tell you tonight. But, Trinity beat us to it."

Tala stepped back to lean into Randell. Her sentry circled her with his arms and she relaxed. "How is the fuck did Trinity pull power from Hell? And she took our elements."

"What?" Mom glanced at all of us. "What are you talking about?"

I shook my head and said softly, "This fight was only a taste of what is coming."

CHAPTER THREE

"Do you want to explain just exactly what the hell you're talking about?" My mom was about as pissed as I'd ever seen her.

Tala sighed and looked at me and Meda. "We combined our power and threw it at Trinity. She had a ball of power ready to throw at us, but the magic in it..." Tala stopped, mouth gaping, at a loss.

I continued for her, voice hard. "The power was from Hell."

Mom's jaw dropped. "How?"

"I'd like to know myself," Meda said.

"Can't you guys call your grandfather?" Harper asked.

"We need to," I murmured. "I couldn't tap into the same power we used when we killed Calista."

"I've been trying," Meda said. "He's blocked us off."

"Fuck," Tala muttered.

"Tala!" My mom looked like she was about to backhand my sarcastic sister. "Language."

"Sorry, Mom," Tala said, but she rolled her eyes at me when Mom looked away. I stifled a grin.

Guilt set in the second I considered grinning. How could I smile at a time like this? We didn't know the count of the dead or injured yet. And more was sure to come.

Mom rubbed her eyes. "This pregnancy," she moaned. "I'm exhausted."

"Mom, go lay down. We can handle this," I stood and took her hands. "Everyone is getting to safety right now. There's nothing you can do."

"Come on," Paw said. "I'll go with you. I've got my phone, they'll call if anything happens." I handed her off to Paw and they walked out of the room, her head bowed and his arm around her.

"It's so hard for her to take a step back." I whirled, delighted to hear the voice of my grandfather. Grandpa Graham stood behind us, arms out. Meda, Tala, and I ran into his arms, like we had since we were small children. Our younger siblings, Griffin and Marly, wiggled between us and pushed us away so they could get their hugs.

We turned from Grandpa Graham to Grandma Sissy. "Hello, darlings," she said, pulling us into hugs. "We're so sorry to have to come home under these circumstances."

"How'd you know to come?" I asked after kissing her soft cheek.

Grandpa handed silver dollars to Griffin and Marly and sent them to play with their nanny. "We started driving this way when we heard about Calista. It took us a few days, but we split the driving and didn't stop."

"I'm happy to see you," Papa said.

"Quin." Grandpa held his hand out. "You've got yourself a right mess here."

"You don't know the half of it." Papa motioned for Grandpa to follow him. "I'll fill you in."

Grandma Sissy followed them out the door, leaving us with Dad. "What can we do?" I asked. It would be much better to stay busy.

Dad looked around, going into High King mode again. "I expect people to start showing up here at any time. Can you three work out a sleeping arrangement? Whatever we have to do, we need room for everyone."

"Of course," Meda said. "We'll do it over here in the corner. Our sentries can help with anything else you need."

"We'll need supplies, food..." Dad's voice trailed off as everyone but my sisters walked with him to his desk.

"Come on," I said, sitting in the corner. Tala ran over to Dad's desk and got a pad of paper and pen.

"How many bedrooms are in here?" she asked.

"Uh, fifteen, I think," I said. We'd explored the house a thousand times over.

"And four rooms big enough to turn into bedrooms," Meda added.

"This room is likely to be the command center." Tala tapped her lip with the pen and squinted her eyes. "It doesn't make sense to be here," she said.

"What are you talking about?" I furrowed my brow. Where else would we go?

"This place is huge, sure, but it's spread out, and there's not enough of anything. But the dorms, however, have more beds, more blankets, more of everything but food."

Meda's face lit up. "You're right. Each floor has sixteen dorms, not to mention a crapton of showers. And, most of the dorms will be abandoned as some families flee until this is over."

I nodded. "We need to tell Dad right now."

We hurried to his desk. He was looking at a list. "What's that?" I asked. Grandpa Graham and Grandma Sissy were nowhere to be seen.

"The dead." Dad looked at us with shocked and sad eyes. "Eight."

Leaning over the desk, Meda read through it. "All sentries."

Dad nodded. "They will be honored. It's a bad week to be a sentry."

I pulled in a deep breath, instinctively reaching for my air to fill my lungs more and faster, but it wasn't there. The sense of loss nearly made me cry again. "Dad, we had an idea."

Meda handed him our list. "We need to move everyone to the dorms."

"Why?" he asked, looking confused. "So many are already here."

"I know, but the dorms have four floors, with sixteen dorms on each of them and eight on ours. Each dorm has bunk beds, except for ours. The school provides the linens, so there's a set of sheets and blankets for every bed already, and we can take some from here, too."

Dad's expression grew more calculating. "Interesting."

"You can make the command center upstairs," I said. "And our rooms will hold far more than they're intended for."

"Hell," Tala said, then ducked her head, looking around for Mom. "I mean, heck, people can sleep in the halls if it comes to it. The square footage is smaller, but it's better equipped to hold all these people."

He cocked his head. "What about food? Those dorms only have small kitchens. The kitchen here is fully stocked and huge."

"If everyone helps, we can easily carry the food over, and Phenex can provide portals if we need to run back and forth."

"Not once the witches are done," he said. "Sterling and his parents are cooking something up with the Dragos."

"The Hightowers and the Dragos are working together?" Meda's voice indicated total disbelief.

"Gino Drago refused to leave." Dad shot me a scathing look. "As a matter of fact, he's insisting he needs to speak with Ami."

I closed my eyes. Maybe if I pretend it wasn't happening, not now at least, it would go away. I had to assume that Gino was the chocolate-eyed witch. And my third mate. And apparently he was connected to the Dragos. Even though I'd heard about their bad reputation, and I preferred to keep my head in the sand. Or a book.

I didn't mind having another mate, not really. I'd known it was coming eventually. But now? Of all times.

"Care to explain that?" he asked me. I didn't even open my eyes, just shook my head no.

"Okay, then. I like this idea. Let's make it happen. Meda, try to contact Phenex and have him get the portal open so we can move supplies. Tala, find Roberto, he's going to be heading up the sentry volunteers. We've had a lot of Collective members volunteer to beef up our fighting ranks." My sisters ran off to find our mate and one of Dad's long-time sentries.

"What can I do?" I asked.

"Go find that damn Italian witch and figure out what he wants. It better not be what I think it is. I don't want you mixed up with the Dragos. They're bad news."

"What do you mean?" I asked suspiciously. "How are they bad news?" I knew the whispers I'd heard, of course, but it was all speculation and rumor.

Dad gave me an assessing look, then rolled his eyes. "Just go see what he wants."

Stopping to look back at him, I couldn't help but wonder what he meant. With no way to know, I walked through the house, searching for Gino or the Hightowers.

After walking half the house and finding nothing but Collective members scurrying everywhere, I found them. Peeking into the library, I saw Sterling and his parents, alone. The coast was clear.

As soon as I stepped inside, Gino walked out from between two stacks, followed by his parents. "Hey, Sterling, I found a spell that might..." His words faded as he saw me. "Ami." A grin spread across his face. "You came."

"Of course I came," I said irritably, channeling Tala. As soon as Gino stepped into sight, my libido launched into overdrive. Nice to see losing my air didn't squash my sex drive. My irritation threatened to turn into sadness again as I thought about my missing air.

Sterling raised his eyebrows at me. He knew it wasn't like me to be brusque.

Ignoring him, I tossed my hair back. "This is my home."

Gino's grin spread. "And a nice home it is."

His mother walked past him, giving me my first full look at her. Her black hair shined in the light from the window, pulled back into a severe bun, making her already-sharp features even more prominent. "Hello," she said smoothly.

By all rights, the polite and proper thing in our society would have been for her to incline her head, even if only a bit.

She didn't. Not that I minded. I didn't have any illusions of grandeur. I was third-born, wouldn't rule, and didn't have any real power of my own to speak of. Besides that, she radiated power. A witch of some magnitude, I wondered how I'd never heard of her.

As I stood in front of her, the severe and powerful woman, my mind blanked, and I couldn't have thought of her last name if my life depended on it. "Nice to meet you, Ms...?"

"Drago," she said, venom dripping from her lips. "And you are?"

My sisters' voices whispered through my mind, an imprint of how they would've handled this situation almost making me smile. Instead, I ducked my head. "Just Ami."

No sense in making her mad. Then she might refuse to help us protect the Collective.

"Well, *just* Ami, why did my son insist we stay until he could speak with you?"

Couldn't her son speak for himself? I didn't mind

being diplomatic and turning the other cheek, but even I had my limit. I raised my gaze and met hers, tired of cowering. "Because he is my mate, Mrs. Drago. And that means he is now tied to me."

She scoffed. "The Drago heir will not be mated to a waif like you."

I shrugged and opened my mouth to tell her to take it up with the ancestors when Gino stepped forward. "Enough," he said in a hard voice.

I looked at him in surprise. Why had he waited so long to come forward? "Took you long enough," I said under my breath.

He heard me. His angry face broke into a wide grin. "I wanted to see how well you could handle my ma. She's a lot."

She rounded on him, probably about to give him a piece of her mind. I put one hand on my hip and ignored her. "And how'd I do?"

"You started off rough, but came through in the second half for a spectacular touchdown."

"A what?" What in the purgatory was a touchdown?

"Nevermind. I can teach you the joys of football at any time. We have the rest of our lives."

"Gino, enough of these games." She ignored me and focused solely on her son. I noticed his dad had retreated to one of the armchairs, beside the High-towers, all three lined up on the sofa, watching in fascination.

"Ma, do you honestly not know who Ami is?" Gino stared his mother down. "Come on, now."

"How should I know who this teenager is?" Mama Drago shot me a scathing look over her shoulder.

Straightening my spine, I drew on every bit of training I'd ever had. Our parents had forced us through etiquette training. Apparently, it was standard practice for vampires to have it, but my sisters gave up on it years before I did. I'd thought it was fun. So had Lilipad. She used to come and sit through the lessons with me sometimes.

Meda had the witchy power, but I wasn't impotent. I trickled magic into my voice and stature. It was more a sense of largeness than anything, but it did the trick.

"My name is Amitola Webb. I am the daughter of Kane, the King of the Vampires, and Jillian, the High Alpha of the Lycans. I am third in line to the throne of the Collective and fifth in line to the throne of the Kingdom of Hell. I am a Princess of the Collective, and that affords me a modicum of respect." I waited a tic before finishing. "Ma'am."

Turning to Gino, I saw Sterling over his shoulder. He was doubled over on the sofa, silently laughing his ass off while his mother smacked at him. "Gino, we should discuss this. Would you care to come with me?"

Turning my gaze to his father, I inclined my head.

Using all the grace my heritage gave me, I turned on my heel and glided from the room. I knew Gino followed me because I heard him snickering all the way.

CHAPTER FOUR

I ducked into the first empty room I came to. It was my Dad's study. After Gino entered, I started to close the door when Noah and Harper appeared in the hall. I scowled at them. "I can talk to him alone."

Harper shook her head. "You're not being alone with him."

"Besides, this affects all of us." Noah nudged Harper inside the room.

Throwing my hands up, I turned, leaving the door open, and faced Gino while crossing my arms. "Tell me why everyone is warning me about you."

One side of his sensual mouth lifted. Magic sparked in his irises. "My family may have gotten a bad reputation over the years. We take care of our own and don't react favorably to those who wish us harm."

I pressed my lips together and stared at him, sure he was being too vague.

Harper snorted beside me. "While the Hightowers have connections to the mob, the Dragos *are* the mob."

Gino cut a glare to Harper then glanced at me with amusement. "That is a rumor. There is no proof."

Studying him for a few moments, I knew he wouldn't open up and spill his dark secrets right then. I'd have to ask around and do my own research. "As you may have noticed, I have two...three other mates." Maybe he'd come clean with a little time.

Gino raised his brows. "Three?"

"Phenex. He's a mate for my sisters too and our center." That was all I was willing to share with Gino at the moment. If he had his secrets, then I'd keep mine. For the time being. "Harper and Noah are also my sentries." I gestured them. "We'll have to learn to find a balance in this relationship."

Gino nodded. "It will be interesting to see how this plays out."

I wasn't so sure I could bond with someone who would lie to me and keep secrets. "If you can't be completely honest with me about something so big, then you can leave. I don't have time to deal with the drama of a mate who keeps secrets from me and our other mates." There was more to tell him about Phenex, but being involved in the mob wasn't something I could handle at this very moment.

Although, I was pretty sure no one could lie to Phenex. The demon had his ways of finding out information. Maybe I'd ask him what he could gather up on Gino.

Without another word, I turned on my heels and left the study. I sensed that Meda and Phenex were back anyway, and I needed to get back to Dad before he came looking for me. I didn't want to deal with explaining to him that I had an Italian witch mobster for a mate. Even though he'd indicated he suspected it.

We were halfway down the hall when Gino caught up to me. "I'm coming with you. I could help with your demonic vampire issue."

I spun on him. "Trinity is now everyone's issue. If we don't stop her, she'll wipe out the entire Collective. That includes the witches, now that Meda and Sterling are mated, and Tala and Fenton, and you are my..." I paused and narrowed my eyes. "Mate." His easy grin widened, both infuriating me and somehow making a puddle form at my core. Darn him.

"Ami."

I closed my eyes briefly at the sound of Papa calling to me. When I opened them, I glared at Gino before facing Papa and forcing a smile. "Yes?"

Papa glanced at Gino and grimaced. "It's time to go."

I started walking again, leaving it up to my mates and Papa to follow. The last thing I needed was to find another mate while preparing for a war.

The great room was packed with people, and I almost couldn't breathe. Reaching for my element, I frowned when it wasn't there and tears formed. Harper took my hand and drew me into her side. Noah stood behind me with his arms around my waist and his head on my shoulder. I relaxed under their touches. I wanted to curl up in my room and get lost in a book, forget the trauma of the day. That wasn't happening any time soon.

Phenex glanced at me with an unreadable stare. He flicked his gaze to Gino and the corners of his mouth tipped down before he turned his attention to my Dad. I would have to talk to the demon about Gino.

Dad stood on top of his desk and addressed the

room. Good thing it was such a big room with vaulted ceilings. "Those who wish to go to the dorms with us are more than welcome. It'll be cramped, but it's safer, better equipped. If you have safe houses, you are welcome to go to them instead. The High Alpha, my fellow High Kings, and I will work with our sentries, my parents, and two of the largest witch circles in the nation to eliminate the threat. For good this time. Trinity has waged war upon us, and I will not hide behind politics. The council is behind the High Alpha's decision to go all-in to protect our people."

Dad pointed to Phenex in the middle of the room. "Phenex is going to put a portal here, if everyone will back up, please." They complied immediately. "It will open on the top floor of the dormitories. Someone is on the other side to assign you a room or possibly a specific bed, depending on your family size." Within moments a large portal opened up.

My sisters and I went through first. We directed people to their rooms, telling them where the linens could be found and that more would be brought over once everyone was settled into their rooms. "Single or family?" I asked a lycan I didn't know very well. "Single," he said gruffly. I smiled, trying to be warm and make him feel comfortable and safe. "Are you a fighter?"

He nodded curtly. "Sentry."

"Sentries are gathering in the last door on the right, top floor." All the sentries would be spread throughout the building to sleep, but they would take their orders from either Randell or Roberto.

A small family came through: a male and female vampire with one young girl. "Vampire family?" I asked politely. The parents nodded. "Vampire families are on the second floor. You move faster than the Lycans. In the event of an attack from below, please have your child use the staircase on that end of the hall to move to the top floor. If you can fight, please use the staircase on the opposite end of the hall to go down to the attack. A sentry will be posted at each staircase. In the event you see no sentry, that means the staircase may not be safe. Understand?" I had to rattle through the information quickly, and I spoke loudly in hopes that the next people waiting behind the portal might hear. Meda and Tala had been doing similarly.

"Yes, thank you, Princess," the mother said with a tiny head bow.

"Ami, please." I squeezed her hand. "We'll get

through this." They moved down the hall, and I faced the next family through.

Lycans didn't have an issue with sharing their quarters with non-family members, because pack was family. Vampires weren't as touchy or cuddly as the Lycans. But for the time being, they seemed to be adjusting. Thank goodness.

It was well into the evening when everyone was settled and food brought in. I worried we'd run out of food before Trinity came back to slaughter us all, but Phenex assured me he could portal us to a grocery store at night. We could leave cash for the items we took. It would be okay.

Finally, free to relax, I stretched out on my bed with my head hanging off the end and stared out the window at the darkening sky. Harper and Noah were in a sentry meeting with my *niswi* and Mom. Since my sisters and I had three mates each, we were allowed to keep our bedrooms to ourselves. Mom and the *niswi* would bunk in the common area. Grandpa and Grandma were in the room Calista used. We'd never let anyone move into it. Yuck.

The bed dipped, and I glanced up, meeting Phenex's dark eyes. He sat cross-legged in the middle of my king-sized bed and held out his arms to me. I sat up and went to him, curling up in his lap with my back pressed to his front.

He took my hands in his and linked our fingers. There was nothing sexual between us, but being in his arms comforted me, brought me a peace I'd never felt before meeting him. "Close your eyes," he ordered in a soft tone.

I did as he said and waited for his guidance into our meditation. We'd done this a few times, and I'd always found clarity afterward.

"I want to try to see if your element was truly taken from you or blocked from your reach."

I nodded. There were so many questions I wanted to ask him but pushed them aside for now. "What do I need to do?"

Please just be a block.

"Open your mind to me and follow my lead." His smooth, deep, slightly accented voice glided into my mind, comforting. I could listen to him speak forever. Sometimes he read to me until I drifted to sleep.

Sensing my sisters, I opened my eyes. Meda and Tala stood inside the doorway watching us.

Phenex said, "Come in and sit."

They crawled on the bed and I shifted so we were in a tight circle, knee to knee. Tala glanced from me to Phenex. "Can you really see if our elements were shielded from our reach?"

"I can." He brought our hands to the middle and my sisters placed theirs on top of our linked fingers. "I need each of you to open your minds. Focus and search for your elements."

Closing my eyes, I searched inside myself for the part that was my element. It was empty and dark, and it made me sad. Where it normally was, a gaping hole taunted me.

I felt alone without my element. After a little while, Phenex appeared there. He pulled me in and soon we stood in the darkness. Then Meda and Tala appeared.

"What do you see?" Phenex asked.

Meda answered first. "Nothing. Except for you guys, everything is black."

"But that isn't nothing."

"What?" Tala frowned, eyeing our demon mate.

Phenex shook his head. "The blackness is what is containing your elements."

Meda's eyes widened. "Like the spell Calista used on the students when she got here."

"Not exactly but close. The power behind the walls is dark, evil. Yet, it's familiar. I can't pinpoint where it is coming from. But someone is pulling

Trinity's strings, or she made a deal with someone as powerful as your grandfather." Phenex growled, and it was the first time outside of a fight that I'd heard him get angry.

"Do you know who that could be?" I asked.

"I have a shortlist. That's not important yet. That will be a job for your grandfather. What is important is figuring out how to end this curse." Phenex pulled out of our linked minds, breaking the connection.

I opened my eyes to see Mom and Dad standing in the doorway. Mom frowned. "What were you doing? Did you hear me talking to you?"

Meda turned on the bed to face our parents. I realized that we hadn't had time to explain how Phenex fit into our mating situation. Meda gave them the brief version. "Phenex is not simply a mate for the three of us. He is our center."

Mom looked puzzled and opened her mouth to question us, but a voice behind her made her turn. Gino stared at me as he spoke. "Phenex is like their familiar, if I understand the mythology behind it. But he's more. He is bound to each of them and will be the catalyst of their powers as they grow, balancing the power of Hell, the elements, and their inner magic."

Dad whirled on Gino. "Where do you fit in?"

Gino calmly held Dad's furious gaze. "I'm Ami's mate. Though, we still have a great deal to work out and a few things to clarify."

Dad stepped closer to Gino, but Mom placed a hand on his chest, stopping him. "Now is not the time. Besides. I know of another couple who were fated mates even though their families and even the law was against it."

I glanced at my sisters. Both of their faces looked strained as we all held in a snicker. Mom was referring to her and Dad, of course. Back when they'd met and the mating urge slammed into them, the councils had forbidden the union of a vampire and a lycan.

Mom turned to us. "Poppy and Lilipad are here. We're having a meeting in the common area."

Meda, Tala, and I jumped up and rushed out of my bedroom. Our grandparents stood in the middle of the room talking with Papa and Paw. I rushed to Poppy and threw my arms around him. "Where have you been?"

He kissed the top of my head as Dad asked, "Yeah, where the fuck were you two? You said you're there for us but when we need you, you don't answer our calls."

I lifted my head to see Poppy's features flash in irritation. "Do you think you are my only child?"

Dad glanced at Lilipad, then Mom before saying, "Um, yeah."

Poppy shrugged. "You are." He laughed at his joke, which made my sisters and I laugh. Poppy made himself laugh more than anyone else. Though this joke was funny, for once.

Normally he was prone to horrible grandpa jokes like, "How do you make holy water? You boil the hell out of it." Then he'd laugh until his face went red, and he ended up gasping.

Mom pinched him and he jumped, rubbing his arm. "This is serious!"

Sighing, Poppy took her hand and pressed a kiss to her fingers. "I know it is." Moving to the kitchen island, he sat on one of the bar stools. Lilipad leaned against him as he explained. "Someone in hell has been plotting against me and starting uprisings for years now. Maybe centuries. It's hard to tell because time moves in weird ways in Hell. Anyway, I can't pinpoint who the source is, but I'm getting closer."

Meda asked, "Do you think it's the same person who is fueling Trinity's power?"

"Trinity?" Poppy sat up and shared a look with Lilipad before turning his attention to Dad. "Kane, if you had mentioned Trinity in your message, we would've come right away."

"That does narrow down who it could be," Lilipad said.

Poppy nodded. "Yes, it does. Oh, damn. I thought she'd be dead by now."

Dad crossed his arms and glared at his father. "Sharing is caring."

A wide smile formed across Poppy's face. "So my son does have my sense of humor. I've never been prouder of you, boy." He shook his head and turned serious. "No, I can't share who I think it is right now. I have to be sure. I also have other shit to deal with. I *am* the ruler of Hell. As a King yourself, you know of the many duties that come with the job. Although you don't torture your people. Plus I have to allow time for my queen." He snaked an arm around Lilipad and nuzzled her neck.

She pushed him away. "You wish." Her voice didn't sound too convincing, though. *Ew. Grandparents shouldn't be allowed to do that in public.*

I crinkled my face and looked at my sisters who mirrored my expression.

My dad's face crumpled like he'd bitten down on a fresh lemon. "Dad!"

"I have your back. If I can't come when you call, I'll send someone right away. I've given Phenex control over the hellhound packs."

Phenex started, and his eyebrows flew up. "Thank you, sir."

"Eh, it's temporary. I can't show favoritism." Poppy glanced around the dorm. "You need to train more of your Collective to fight and prepare for a war more bloody than any of us has ever seen. But you can't do it here."

Dad sighed. He looked tired and annoyed with Poppy. "We just got everyone settled, and this is the best we've got. Do you have anywhere safer in mind?"

"I do." Poppy stood and smiled at everyone. "I have access to a private island. It's safe and no one knows about it."

"An island?" Dad looked at Poppy suspiciously. "How is an island safer than here?"

Poppy rolled his eyes. "It's not in this realm." He winked at my sisters and me. "*Duh.*"

CHAPTER FIVE

"Poppy, can you help us?" I asked. Surely he could do something. "She took our elements."

He looked shocked, then furious. "Explain."

Meda held out her hand. "We can't reach our elemental powers. It's like they're not there."

"Also," I added. "When she first attacked, before she took our powers, I connected to my sisters and made a huge ball of energy, magic, and elemental power. I wanted to add the power of Hell to it, but it was closed to me. I couldn't access it."

Lilipad touched my arm. "I'm sorry, darling. You must've felt helpless."

"I had our other powers to lean on." I took her

hand. "But now, without our elements, we're vulnerable."

Poppy walked across the dorm and looked out the window at the darkened campus. All lights had been shut off. The vampire and lycan sentries saw better without the artificial lights altering their vision. The witches that had turned up to help, mostly a few close friends of the Hightowers or parents of the students, were safely ensconced on the top floor with the sentries.

Phenex stood. "Sir, their powers are still linked to them. They haven't been removed. But they're being used by someone else, and the triplets can't reach them at all. To them, it's total darkness. A black hole where their power used to thrive."

Poppy nodded. "Only a few people could do that. And only one would..." He sniffed. "Well, anyway. I'll deal with that. That's the best way I can help, besides the island. Phenex, if you'll come with me, I'll take you there."

Poppy hugged and kissed us all, then gave Lilipad a lingering kiss. "I'll see you soon."

She patted her hair when he pulled away, clearly flustered. Phenex hugged my sisters and me and kissed us all on the forehead. I felt a tiny zing of power trickle into me. Nothing major, just his way of saying goodbye. Like a hug or kiss.

Phenex took Poppy's hand and they disappeared.

Dad arched an eyebrow at Lilipad. "I thought you couldn't stand him?"

She straightened her suit coat. Lilipad always dressed to the nines. She said it made her feel like she had a semblance of control in a chaotic world. When we were young, we all thought that meant Hell was a massive fiery room full of demons running around screaming and wreaking havoc.

Our parents finally let us visit when we turned thirteen. We couldn't have been more wrong. Hell was hot and fiery, the realm containing it being so. But it was set up more like a giant office building, except the floors went down, and never ended. Poppy swore he knew every level, every floor, every room, but I wasn't so sure.

Lilipad sniffed at my dad. "Why don't you worry about yourself?"

Dad grinned. "Sure, mom. Whatever you say."

Paw stood and clapped his hands together. "Are we doing this island thing?"

Lilipad nodded. "I've been there. It's in a realm Luce created. As far as I know, only he and I, and now Phenex have ever been there."

Creating a realm took a ridiculous amount of power. "When did he make a whole realm?"

"Oh, hundreds of years ago. It was one of the things he did to try to woo me." She rolled her eyes. "The fool."

Lilipad was very secretive about why she resisted Poppy so hard. She said it had to do with how he treated her when they first met. Dad told us once that all he knew was that Poppy wasn't happy with the way things were run in heaven, he rebelled, ended up leaving, and the first thing he did was make Lilipad. He'd never been told anything more.

Whatever happened between them, it had been obvious Lilipad had feelings for him now. I wondered how long it would take them to sort it all out.

"What can we expect?" Meda asked, going into organizer and leader mode. She couldn't keep her room clean to save her life, but give her a group of people to save and she turned into Joan of Arc. "What sort of accommodations, provisions?"

"Oh, he'll update it for you before you get there. I'm sure there will be plenty of food. Don't worry. Just come. If there's anything you need once there and you can't reach us, Phenex will be able to create a portal."

She made the rounds, hugging everyone, starting with my Dad and ending with me. "Sweet girl," she whispered. "You and I are much alike. When I was young..." She sighed and wiped her eyes. My heart beat faster. They all worried about me so often. I wasn't strong like them, and they thought I was spaced out. In reality, I liked to read and always had so many stories floating around in my head. I never missed anything going on around me but didn't always see the need to involve myself. Though, they were right about me not being very strong. That was my sisters.

Lilipad squeezed me again. "Don't worry about what is to come. You're going to surprise yourself."

I had no idea what she was talking about, but I smiled and hugged her tight. "Love you, Lilipad."

She kissed my forehead, the way Phenex had, but no jolt of power this time. Then she disappeared.

"Why can a vampire disappear?" Sterling asked. He hadn't grown up around our family, so he probably still had a lot of questions.

"Now that she's officially situated on the throne as the Queen of Hell, Poppy gave her nearly the same amount of power he has," Meda explained to her mate.

"Nearly?" He raised his eyebrows. "I can't

imagine trying to give you *nearly* as much power. You'd kill me."

Everyone laughed. Meda most definitely would have killed him for something like that.

"My mother is a complicated creature. If not for Dad, she would've been dead a couple thousand years ago."

Randell whistled. "I didn't know that."

"Right, well," Dad said, standing from the bar stool he'd perched on to talk to Poppy. "We've got more work to do tonight. Meda, Tala, Ami. Each of you take a floor, take your mates and sentries. Notify everyone that we're moving to the island. They can bring only what they can carry. Everything else will be provided."

He turned to Sterling. "Can you spread the word among the witches? There will be very little protection from the Collective left on Earth, and those that stay will be in hiding. If they need help, we won't be able to provide any. But they are welcome to come."

Sterling nodded. "I'll tell my parents and the Dracos."

"Thanks. We'll start the phone chain and reach out to those that didn't come to stay at the dorms. Everyone must be ready to go at first light."

We dispersed to do our assigned jobs. Harper, Noah, and I went down to the first floor and updated everyone down there. Mostly individuals, vampires and Lycans without any family. One room held a family of witches, and the back corner four-bedroom dorm held some lycan overflow. Elijah's family was there.

"Hey." I gave his mom a big hug. "How are you holding up?"

She shrugged. "Okay, I guess. This is a lot to take."

"I know. But I've come to give good news."

His dad walked closer, and I explained about the island. "Be ready to go at first light. Top floor. We'll have a portal."

"Ami," Sarah said, following me into the hall. She pulled the door close. "How bad is this, really?"

I considered my words carefully. She was grieving deeply, but I didn't want to lie to her.

"It's bad, honestly. But it's not the end of the world. We'll get through it."

I pulled her into a hug and tried again to reach for my air. Nothing.

"See you in the morning?" I asked.

She nodded. "Have a good night, Ami."

Theirs was the last family to tell on the floor.

Harper and Noah waited for me at the stairs at the end of the hall. "You okay?" Noah asked.

"Yeah," I said. "I wish I could fix this." He put his arm around me, and we followed Harper upstairs. Everyone else had returned.

I looked at my mates and couldn't help but wonder where Gino was and if he was thinking about me. "Let's get some sleep. It'll be another long day tomorrow."

CHAPTER SIX

When we reached the top floor, Noah pressed a kiss to my lips. "I'm on watch." He pulled back and his green eyes brightened as his wolf looked out at me, most likely sensing my sadness and worry about the future.

I squeezed his hand. "Go. I'll be fine."

He glanced at Harper then nodded before leaving. Harper linked our hands and tugged me into the dorm. We crossed the common area to my room without the parental units noticing. If they did, they didn't acknowledge us. Thank Lucifer.

Once inside the bedroom, Harper closed the door and locked it. I met her desire-filled gaze and squeezed my thighs together. I ached with need for both my mates. Gino wasn't here yet. Even though the urge to have him buried deep inside me was strong, unease overcame desire when it came to him.

Harper moved forward, watching like I was her prey. Excitement filled me, warm tingles racing through my body. I was alpha because both my parents were. However, I didn't need to dominate all the time. I learned pretty quickly that I liked submitting to my mates. It was the only time I could let my guard down and turn over control to them.

When Harper's fangs lengthened enough to peek out from her upper lip, I groaned and cupped my breasts over my t-shirt. She watched the movement, her bright blue eyes darkening with desire. A lower growl escaped her, fueling my desires.

Harper and I had always been close friends. But once the mating urge slammed into us, that friendship bloomed in lust and need. She was my heart, as was Noah.

Stopping in front me, Harper brushed my hands away and pulled my shirt over my head, tossing it to the floor. A wicked smile formed when she noticed I was wearing her bra. A black lacey one I loved. "I might be jealous that my bra looks better on you than me."

"It's very comfortable." I grinned at her.

"I know." She dipped her head and kissed the top curve of my breast. "I want to mark you."

My breath came out in a rush with a groan following. The thought of Harper biting me almost made me come right then. "Yes." It definitely made my panties soaked.

Harper reached around me to unhook her bra then slid the straps down my shoulders. A whimper escaped me. Why was she torturing me with her slow seduction? "Harper," I warned.

She laughed, knowing good and well that I'd turn alpha if I needed to. In this case, when I wanted something bad enough.

Bending her head, she licked one nipple, then the other as she unbuttoned my jeans. The cool air of my bedroom tickled my wet nipples, and they tightened to nubs.

The zipper was next. After she slid the denim over my hips, she pushed my shoulders so I fell backward onto the bed, giggling.

Fire ignited in her eyes. Flames of passion that brightened her eyes. We locked gazes as she removed my jeans and panties.

Harper pressed a kiss on the inside of my leg and nipped at my skin. I cried out in pleasure then grabbed the pillow and placed it over my face. No need to alert my parents on what we were doing. Although, they probably already knew. Sometimes our excellent hearing meant we heard far more than we wanted to. I was pretty sure my parents had soundproofed their room for just such a reason, because my sisters and I hadn't ever heard anything icky from there.

Pushing that gross thought away, I focused on my mate. Harper covered me with her mouth, sucking and licking. I bucked my hips, riding the wave of pleasure exploding inside me. With strong hands, she held my hips in place, reaching around my legs to spread me wide open to her tongue.

I let my legs fall to the side, giving her as much access as possible and forcing myself not to buck.

It freed up her hands. Keeping her mouth on my clit, she slid two fingers inside and rolled them around, exploring and enjoying my body.

For all that was unholy, the woman had a talented mouth. Her tongue ring slid against my nub, the smooth ball pressing and adding a powerful zing of pleasure.

I rolled my hips in rhythm with her, and she fucked me with her fingers, picking up speed and going deeper with each thrust, then curling them first in one direction, then the other. She found the perfect spot, focusing on it until I bit down on the pillow as the orgasm slammed into me, causing my body to spasm.

Harper crawled up my body, nipping at my flesh along the way. When she straddled my waist, I flipped us over to flatten her on the bed.

With fast fingers, I removed her clothes a lot quicker than she had mine. By the wicked smile that formed on her face, she enjoyed my eagerness. Her jeans caught on her ankles, so I kissed the soles of her feet as I disentangled her from the material.

She giggled until she was naked, and my hands were well away from her sensitive feet.

Once I stripped her bare, I crawled up, so I hovered over her while cupping her. Sliding my fingers through her slick folds, I teased her clit before I entered her, her low moans turning me on again. I thrust my fingers in and out while rubbing her clit with my thumb.

Lying at her side, my fingers still drawing moans and gasps from her lips, I captured her mouth in a raw kiss, thrusting my tongue inside her mouth and tangling it with hers. My hand moved faster, her sounds and overheated body readying me for another orgasm.

Harper threaded her fingers in my hair and

curled them into fists as she rode my hand and pulled my head to the side. Then she struck. Her fangs sank into my throat, and I rolled my body to hers, feeling our heated flesh press against each other, my arm trapped between us as I continued my movements.

As the bite-induced orgasm washed through me, my fangs lengthened, and I bit her shoulder. Damn. She was amazing. My mate.

She tasted sweet and rich. Her blood coated my tongue and slid down my throat. I picked up the tempo, fingering her as she pushed me to the side, rolling with me and entering me again. We connected as one. It was the only place I wanted to be. Harper was mine, and I loved her.

As soon as the thought merged so did the threads of our mating bond. I hesitated and wondered if this was what Harper wanted. She must have felt my hesitation because she pulled her fingers out of me, hooking her legs around my waist and wrapping me in her arms, holding me to tell me she was all in. Opening up, I allowed the bond to form until it snapped into place, binding us together.

Then we both completed our orgasms at the same time. Our pleasure bounced between us, intensifying our release.

When the last shudders left our bodies, we

curled into each other. Harper played with my hair, twirling the black stands with her fingers. "I love you, A."

I squeezed her. "Love you too, H."

My sisters and I sometimes called each other by our first initial and Harper and I started to do it somewhere along the way. It fit us.

Harper kissed my lips. "Get some sleep. I'll be here until it's time for me to relieve Noah."

I nodded. I was tired despite being anxious about the pending war and the safety of my people. She hadn't needed to tell me to sleep. It was coming for me anyway.

Movement on the bed made me open my eyes, fear gripping my chest and squeezing. Noah's smooth voice settled over me. "Just me."

Staring into his eyes, I cupped his cheeks. "What time is it?"

He bent down and kissed me, letting his lips linger for a little bit. "Late. Well, early for you. It's two."

He stripped down to his black boxer briefs then climbed under the covers with me. A wicked grin formed as I snuggled against him. "You and Harp are killing me. I've told her I wanted to watch you two. The thought..." He cut off his statement with a growl.

Needing a distraction from my worrying thoughts, I traced circled on his chest, then walked my fingers down to the waistband of the boxers. "Maybe next time you can watch and join in."

A low growl was his reply as he rolled to pin me to the bed. "That sounds like a plan." He nuzzled my neck, then jerked his head up. Frowning, he said, "You bonded with her."

Dread churned in my gut. "Are you angry? I know we haven't talked about it. But it felt right at the time for Harp and me to bond."

He framed my face and kissed my nose. "No. I could never be mad at you. Frustrated, maybe." He paused and squeezed me. "I'm envious."

There was a tease in his tone that made me relax. I draped my arms around his neck, then my legs around his waist. "Don't be. We can now if you want."

His wolf flashed in his eyes. "As much as I want to, I don't want to do it just because you and Harper did." He brushed the hair from my face. "We'll do it on our own time when we both know it's the right time."

I cupped him over his boxers, and he pressed into my hand with a moan. "I do want to mark you. Make that Italian witch know exactly what he's missing by not coming clean with us."

Gino. I frowned. "I'm going to talk to Phenex about him once we all get settled on the island."

Noah dipped his head and kissed her throat. "Good idea. If anyone could dig out someone's darkest secrets, it's the demon."

I groaned as Noah bit the curve of my neck on the opposite side Harper did. My body jerked and pleasure crashed over me. Noah gripped my wrist and pulled my hand away from his hard cock to hold it above my head. Then he jerked his boxers down and thrust inside me.

I cried out at the feel of him rapidly stretching me. He started moving, slowly at first then increasing his thrusts, each one taking him deeper inside. I scored his back with my nails, not caring if I left scratches, marking him as mine.

"Come," he whispered without releasing my neck.

His words were a command I was happy to obey. My climax pulled me over the edge of bliss. Noah followed with his orgasm.

His breaths came in pants as he let go then watched me behind a desire-drunk gaze. I kissed him. "Love you."

He blinked and stared at me for a moment before smiling. "Love you too." It was the first time either of us had said it.

That was when I felt it. The threads of a mating bond between us. Smiling I framed his face. "Apparently the time is right for the bond to form."

"Apparently." He kissed my lips, let it linger a bit before he kissed my nose. All the while the bond strengthened. "I love feeling you inside me."

"Me too." I let out a gasp as the mating link between grabbed hold and snapped into place.

Lying beside me, he pulled me close, holding me as I drifted off to sleep. Whatever was coming, at least I had them and my family.

As soon as I stepped foot onto the sandy beach behind Mom and looked around, my jaw dropped. Freezing in place, Meda and Tala jostled against me as they tried to come through.

"Ami, you know we can't touch the edges of the portal. Move," Tala said testily as she rubbed her arm. She must've gotten close.

"Sorry," I exclaimed, and scampered farther down the beach. They followed, and I glanced back to see their faces were as awestruck as my own.

"Welcome," a voice exclaimed in an exotic accent. "I am here to service your every need." It was difficult to hear him over the sound of the waves.

We turned toward the water to see a man

walking from the ocean. His red, scaly skin sparkled in the mid-morning sun.

My sisters and I were supposedly the three rarest creatures on the face of the Earth. We'd met creatures of all shapes and sizes in our lives. The world wasn't only made up of vampires, Lycans, and humans. It was full of fantastical and mystical creatures.

But this guy? He was far beyond anything any of us had ever seen.

"Hello," Meda said hesitantly. Our mates moved forward, putting their bodies slightly in front of our own as our *niswi* moved toward the red creature.

"I am Delphin," the creature stated. "Your sire has entrusted your comfort and care to me."

He gestured inland, behind us. "We have anticipated many of your coming needs, but as water-dwelling creatures, we may have fallen short. Please do not hesitate to ask for anything you need. It will be provided with the utmost haste."

My parents stepped forward cautiously and introduced themselves. The red man bowed his head. "My people have been given a safe home in this realm. In exchange, we care for your sire when he stays here."

The Collective poured through the portal, filling

the beach with shocked vampires, Lycans, and witches. Soon we had a clogged area right in front of the portal.

Meda nodded to Tala and me. "Let's move this along while they talk to Mr. Lizard over there."

"I think it's more like Mr. Fish," Tala murmured.

"What if he's a mermaid?" My world would be complete if mermaids lived in it. "I hope he is."

Tala snorted and held up her arms. "Okay, people, move on down the beach. Make room, now. Lots more people coming through."

We helped people shuffle along the beach until everyone was there. The last of the sentries, charged with bringing up the rear, walked through, and Phenex closed the portal. He eyeballed the strange man speaking to our parents as he joined us. "I counted as they went through. We told everyone to be there by nine, and it took until nine-thirty to get everyone through, so I closed it."

Meda nodded. "It's all we could do." She cocked her head at him. "Can you make a portal small enough to peek through?"

He nodded. "Yes, it's useful for spying."

"Are hellhounds the only creatures that can make these portals?" I asked.

"No, anyone with the power of Hell can," he said.

"Including you, once you learn to fully embrace your powers."

I thought I already had learned to fully embrace my powers. "Oh."

The crowd on the beach grew restless. They didn't appreciate being confined to the sand when there was obviously so much to explore inland.

"Hey," I whispered. "We need to hurry them up." I nodded toward our parents and the mermaid. *Please be a mermaid.*

"Yeah. Come on." Meda turned toward them, and our mates still blocking us from being in the direct sight of the creature they didn't know—or trust. "Oh, move, you overprotective nannies."

Tala snorted and pushed through them, chuckling. "Nannies." Randell raised his eyebrows at her as he watched her walk past him but didn't contradict her.

"Hey, sorry to break up the talk, but the kids are restless," Tala said as she approached our parents.

"Tala, Meda, Ami, this is Delphin. He is the ruler of the merfolk that live in this realm." My cheeks flamed and blood pumped harder as Dad inclined his head to Delphin, so my sisters and I did the same.

"It's a pleasure to meet you," I said breathlessly.

"I'd love to hear more about your people while we're here."

Delphin smiled, and his teeth were all pointed like my fangs. Ouch. "I'll send my daughter to make your acquaintance when you're settled." He returned his gaze to my parents. "I must return to the water. We cannot stay long without suffering consequences. The magic is strong and will hold as long as you need to stay."

Mom thanked him again, and he walked into the sea, disappearing under the waves. "Wow," I whispered. The desire to follow him was strong and didn't abate until I felt a hand on my shoulder.

Noah. I turned and looked up at him. "Yes?"

"You looked like you were going to go for a swim," he said ruefully.

"Don't think I wouldn't have if I thought I could get away with it."

Mom laughed. "I knew as soon as I saw him that we'd have trouble out of you."

"Did you know?" I asked.

She shook her head. "Never imagined such a creature could exist."

"I knew," Dad said. "Why do you think I never told you?"

"Because you would've never seen me again?" I asked and gave him a cheeky grin.

"Exactly. Come on, let's get everyone moving."

He held his hands up and moved toward the crowd. "Where is Sterling? Or Fenton?"

Fenton stood behind Randell. Slightly shorter, he was hidden from view. "What's up?" he asked, walking into Dad's path. "Sterling is helping his parents."

"Can you amplify my voice?"

Fenton put his fingers on Dad's neck. "There. It'll last about two minutes."

"Thanks," Dad said, and the word boomed over us, assaulting our ears and making the people closest to him wince.

"Sorry," he whispered, but the magic still made the whisper unbearably loud, even with the sound of the water.

Mom turned him away from us. "Fenton, have you ever done that before?" she asked.

Fenton's eyes widened. "No."

Randell's gleeful face made us all chuckle as he teased his friend. Mate? Did our guys call each other mate? It was a question for a calmer moment. "I think you overdid it, brother," Randell said through his chuckles.

"Try to speak softly," Mom murmured to Dad. "Or you'll overwhelm their sensitive hearing."

"Hello, all," Dad said in a hushed tone. If anyone waited on us on the other side of the—apparently huge—island, they knew we were here now.

"Sorry about the volume," he continued, shooting Fenton a glare. Fenton shrugged.

"There are merfolk here, and they're friendly. They have strong magic. They've worked at my father's orders to make this place as inviting and comfortable as possible. To the left," Dad said and pointed inland toward three large buildings. "You'll find what amounts to hotels. We don't have staff or help, but you'll find clothes downstairs that change size to fit their owner. There is plenty of food in the kitchens that won't run out no matter how much we cook. He did say it's mostly seafood and fruits grown on the island. Vampires, we will set up a donation schedule between the Lycans and witches."

A few faces darkened at the idea of sharing blood, but we'd end up with enough volunteers, mainly from the younger Collective members. My mom leaned over and whispered something to Randell, but with the sound of the water and murmurs of the crowd, I didn't catch it. He tapped

Harper on the shoulder, and they walked toward the hotels.

"To the right should service our entertainment and training needs. He mentioned pools, golf, and other sports options, as well as an advanced training facility. We will be setting up a training schedule for every able-bodied Collective member. Which is nearly all of you, so be prepared. In a war against Hell, we must all prepare."

Most of the crowd nodded, looking angry and ready to fight. I was glad to see they were willing to stand up for themselves. "If anyone needs anything, find a sentry and explain. We will do whatever we can to provide for your every need and most of the wants as well."

He moved his arms in a waving motion. "Go find your rooms and settle in."

The crowd turned toward the paths leading away from the beach and hurried inland. "They seem excited," I said.

"They're safe here, most of them have their entire family here. Nothing else to do but try to enjoy it," Papa said. "Hell, I'm a little excited myself. When was the last time we went on a vacation?"

Tala snorted. "I think we were thirteen."

"Exactly. We have a lot of work to do, preparing

for whatever Trinity is going to throw at us, but that doesn't mean we can't enjoy the setting." Paw shook his head. "At least, they can. We have strategies to plan and you girls have magic to learn."

My shoulders sank. It had been easy to push it to the back of my mind and focus on the beauty of the island. But all it meant was that we'd be working in a different setting. The work still had to be done.

When the last of the crowd went up the paths, we followed. Meda, Tala, and I went first, followed by our parents, our younger brothers and sisters, who had returned from traveling with Grandpa and Grandma, then all our mates and sentries.

Without warning, Tala jumped and laughed.

"What?" I asked.

"Randell popped into my head without warning and it startled me," she said between chuckles. "Now he's teasing me about it." She didn't speak for a moment. "There, I told him what would happen if it didn't stop." Meda and I laughed with her, knowing exactly what she meant.

Turning her head over her shoulder to look back at the rest of our crowd, she said, "Randell said we're on the top floor in the far-right building."

At the next path split, we went right, toward the innermost hotel. "Is that why they left?" I asked.

"Yes, I asked them to go find us appropriate rooms that could be defended," Mom said.

"You think we'll need defense here?" I asked, worry lining my stomach.

"I think we, and especially you three, need defense everywhere." She stepped forward and squeezed my shoulder. "Sorry, baby. It came with the crown."

I'd never wear that crown. Why did it have to apply to me?

Even as I thought it, I felt bad. I'd never leave Meda to fight alone. Or Tala.

"How much power did it take to make this place?" Meda asked.

Fenton, bringing up the rear with our other mates and sentries, stepped forward. "The realm itself would've taken a considerable amount."

"He did that years ago," Dad said.

"Then all this stuff on it? Not so much, especially if the merfolk helped." Fenton straightened his glasses. "It's a matter of conjuring."

We stepped off the path and onto a boardwalk. The crowd was already spread all over the place. Some still worked their way into the hotels, but others had opted to go check out the amenities first. Just from our vantage point, I saw an arcade, what looked like unmanned food stands, and shops full of clothes to our far right. Closer to the right several pools sat waiting for occupants. Slides, swings, and all manner of fun pool toys waited on the kids.

"I wonder if any homeowners are waking up this morning and wondering where in the hell their pools went?" I asked.

My family all laughed. "That's an awkward call to the insurance company," Fenton said.

"What's an insurance company?" Tala asked. Fenton gave her a blank stare. I knew what it was thanks to the human books I loved to read. "I'll tell you later," he promised. "Let's go put our stuff up." We headed toward the hotel, passing Collective members as they hurried back out of the building.

"I guess they already put their stuff in their rooms and want to play," I said with a chuckle as a tiny vampire girl pulled her intimidating-looking father toward the shops. "Come on, Daddy, I want to look for a princess dress."

He nodded his head as she dragged him past us.

The *niswi* chuckled as they saw his plight. Dad patted the man's shoulder as he went by. "It doesn't get any easier, my friend."

"Hey," Tala said. "We're a friggin' delight."

The *niswi* laughed harder.

"What's so funny?" Meda asked in mock outrage. "We weren't difficult."

I stayed silent, enjoying the sight of our *niswi* clutching each other in their laughter. There wasn't much to laugh about at the moment. They needed it. Mom rolled her eyes. "Girls, go ahead and get settled. I'll get these buffoons moving."

We flipped our hair in unison, a move we'd practiced over the years. Our mates detached themselves from the crowd and joined us.

The outside of the hotel was fairly plain, a large blond-brick square. The inside was another story entirely. Fountains in the lobby welcomed us into the building we'd be staying in for the foreseeable future. A sign past the fountains gave directions. The kitchens were on the main level. Each floor had several suites of rooms. A wardrobe room was also on this floor, as well as a library.

Oh, a library. I know where I want to go.

"Well, I guess we'll lose Ami soon," Meda said, pointing at the word library on the sign.

"I'll try to resist," I said softly. Noah put his arm around me. "No need to resist. Let's get settled, and I'll go to the library with you happily."

Tala and her guys were already headed to the stairs, so we followed.

Our rooms were perfect. Big windows gave a great view of the ocean. Randell and Harper found us the largest suite, so they said. It had bedrooms for the three of us and connected to another suite with rooms for Mom and the *niswi*, Grandpa Graham and Grandma Sissy, and our younger brother and sister. I needed to spend some time with them. They'd traveled with our grandparents all summer and we'd barely seen them.

"Come on," Harper said. "I snagged us a room with a balcony." She tugged me through the large bedroom and past the bathroom door. I peered in to see a giant tub. Nice.

The balcony wasn't large, but she couldn't wait to show me. "I keep picturing you out here with a book, snuggled in one of the big, soft blankets from the bed."

I looked back to see the two enormous beds were made up with a quilt, then draped at the end two fuzzy throw blankets. "It sounds amazing," I said, pulling her toward me. She wrapped her arms around me, and we looked at the ocean.

"At least we're safe here." She kissed the top of my head. "That's what matters."

CHAPTER EIGHT

No matter how safe we all felt, we couldn't hide in the paradise island realm forever. I rested my head on Harper's shoulder and looked out over the beach. "It's beautiful." The crashing waves called to me. They must've been unbearable to Tala.

Harper nodded. "It is."

I took her hand and tugged her toward the door, unable to contain my excitement much longer. Besides, I needed something to think about other than the war against Trinity. When we stepped into the living room area of our suite, I found Noah with his head stuck in the refrigerator. "Noah, let's go explore."

Instantly he stood by my side. Smiling, I led my mates to the main floor of the hotel. As much as I wanted to get lost in that amazing library, I wanted to see the island a bit and pretend for a few moments that a psycho bitch didn't want to kill us all. And that I wasn't missing a huge part of myself.

When I stepped outside a breeze swirled around me. I inhaled and closed my eyes as a longing in my chest made me ache. Although I felt the air kissing my skin, I couldn't connect with it. Sadness filled me. Both Harper and Noah felt it and wrapped an arm around me. We were bonded now and could feel each other's emotions. They knew I was missing my air.

Harper kissed my cheek. "We'll find a way to break the curse and get your elements back."

I nodded and leaned into her. Noah cupped my face. "I bet Phenex is working on that now."

"He is." I knew Phenex was because—even though he didn't show it—he was pissed that Trinity was able to take my sisters' and my elements in the first place. "Come on. Let's go explore."

We met up with many of the Collective families and chatted with them while watching the kids play. As one of the Collective princesses, it was my duty to know my people. Normally, I was the one who liked to hide out with a book. Large crowds made me nervous. However, right then my people needed everyone in my family and the sentries to be visible and willing to help without hesitation.

Of course, I never saw Meda or Tala walking around, helping the people acclimate to their temporary home.

By the time Harper, Noah, and I made it back to the hotel, I was peopled out.

My mates noticed, of course, and directed me to the library. I lost myself in the fantasy section, stacking book after book in a pile to take back to my room until I felt *his* presence. Glancing up from a book, I locked eyes with Gino. He raked his gaze over me and darn if it didn't feel like a physical caress.

I suppressed my shudder as he stalked toward me. His sensual lips slowly lifted into a wicked smile.

Forcing my attention back to my book, I tried to appear like I wasn't affected by him. But it was so darn hard. His scent wrapped around me and made my lady parts ache for his touch.

Harper and Noah made their presences known, obviously sensing my emotions through our bond. They each took a seat on the arms of my comfy chair —Harper on my left and Noah on my right.

Gino watched them with amusement and sat in

the chair across from us. "We do need to talk about this mating."

Yes, I knew that. And right then seemed like a good time because who knew what would happen in the coming days. "I know nothing about you. My dad is obviously against this. Why is that?"

Harper added, "Or why not start with the rumors that your family is the witch mob?"

Gino flicked his gaze to Harper then back to me. "My family does have a reputation. We don't engage in illegal activities. We take care of our own and punish those who deserve it."

I raised my brows. "Please enlighten me."

A ghost of a smile formed on his face, making me react viscerally. *Darn him.* I squeezed my thighs together.

"Witches are not without their rogues. Magic can be an addictive power, especially dark magic. We take care of the rogues, eliminating the threat before it gets out of hand." He shrugged as if it was that simple.

Yeah, right. There was so much more to his words. "So, your family is like the rogue hunters of the witches?"

"Not *technically.*" He leaned forward in his seat

and my wolf danced around, eager to get close to him. "We don't hunt them. If a situation is brought to our attention we take care of the problem. Many times that is done as a favor."

"So people come to you with a problem and for a favor, you take care of it." I frowned. That sounded way too familiar. "That's pretty much mob behavior."

Gino's mouth lifted in a full, panty-wetting smile. "But isn't your grandfather the original mob boss?"

Yeah. He had a point there. *Darn him.*

Standing, Gino held out his hand. "Come walk with me?"

Harper and Noah tensed. I knew they didn't want me out of sight. After all, they'd been my sentries since we were young teens. Mom and the *niswi* had thought it'd be a good idea to place a few sentries with my sisters and I that were close to our age. That way we'd be friends as they trained with us and with the other sentries to protect us.

Standing, I faced them. "I'll be fine. Gino is my mate and so can't harm me."

He could, but if he wanted to stay alive, he wouldn't. Plus Poppy would make sure Gino's soul suffered after death.

Shaking out of that last thought, I focused on Noah and Harper. "I'll see you at dinner?"

They both glared at Gino but nodded. Harper said, "We're going to check in with Randall and get some training in."

She stood and pressed a kiss to my lips, lingering for a moment before stepping back. Noah drew me into a hug. I rested my cheek to his chest and sighed. His wolf was restless but calmed as I hugged him. Lifting my gaze to his I said, "I'll be okay."

Noah grunted but kissed my forehead before releasing me. Then they left the library.

"They care for you." It wasn't a question.

Nodding, I faced Gino. "They're my mates and the bond is new."

Gino nodded and held out his arm, bent at the elbow, to me. "Shall we?"

I looped my arm in his and allowed him to direct me out of the library. A walkway out the back of the hotel led to a beautiful garden. It was something out of a fairytale. Blue, purple, yellow, and red flowers bloomed all around us, and they seemed to sparkle in the sunlight. "This is amazing." I touched a pale green flower and it shrank in on itself. When I drew my hand away, it bloomed again. "They're magical?" We had a small magical garden at home, maintained by a witch-friend of my mom's, but it was nothing this grand.

"I thought you'd like it," Gino said with a smile.

I narrowed my eyes at him. "Are you trying to seduce me?"

His internal magic sparked in his chocolate eyes. "Is it working?"

Tugging me to him, he wrapped an arm around me, pressing our bodies together. I sucked in a breath at the contact as my body lit up like a Christmas tree. Flattening my palms to his chest, I locked gazes with him. "Maybe."

A low chuckle escaped him. Then his expression turned serious, but he didn't let go of me. "You're mine, Ami."

As he was mine, but I didn't tell him that. Pushing against his chest, I said, "We'll see." When his grip didn't budge, I raised an eyebrow.

He released me, not that he had a choice, and I remained where I was instead of putting distance between us like I made him think I wanted. Actually what I wanted was to strip him naked and...

Shaking out of that thought, I stared into his dark gaze. There was a question bugging me since I saw him at Elijah's funnel. "How do you know Elijah's family?"

Something dark clouded his features, and he turned so I stared at his profile. An ache formed in my chest. Several moments went by before Gino answered. "Elijah was my lover." His raw voice held truth.

I opened my mouth and closed it. "I didn't know he was seeing anyone." Let alone, my mate. Did that mean he was gay? What if he wasn't sexually attracted to me. I already had a bond like that with Phenex. It might not have been so bad, except for the fact that I was horny for him.

"Elijah wasn't open with his sexuality. We weren't fated mates as far as I knew, but I cared for him deeply." The break in his voice triggered my tears.

When I sniffed, Gino snapped his attention back to me. I waved him off then hugged my waist. "My sisters and I loved Elijah like a brother. He was family and our sentry."

Before I took my next breath, Gino enveloped me in his arms. I hugged him back, burying my face into his shirt. "He saved my mom's life."

He lifted my chin so our gazes locked. "It was his job. All of us knew if it came down to it, he'd do what it took to protect the High Alpha and her princesses."

"It still doesn't make it any easier." My vision blurred.

Gino swiped a tear from my cheek, then slid his hand to the base of my neck. He lowered his head, and I held my breath in anticipation of how his lips would feel. When he brushed his lips against mine, I groaned and flattened my body to his while standing on my toes. Desire flood my senses, making me dizzy with need. My wolf howled in triumph. My inner vampire wanted to taste him.

All of us were thrilled he wasn't gay. Bi we could deal with.

Sliding his hands down my back and cupping my butt cheeks, he lifted me. I wrapped my legs around his waist as he slipped his tongue into my mouth. I met it halfway with my own.

I sensed Meda as she approached and broke the kiss. Gino and I glanced at her, noting the smirk on her face. Wiggling, I loosened my legs from around Gino, and he lowered me to the ground.

Meda studied Gino for a moment before looking at me. "Phenex wants to work with us on learning to connect our powers without our elements."

I made a face before I realized had. "I thought we were going to get settled in."

"And we are." Meda turned and walked away. I

could tell that she wasn't happy about training right then either.

With a sigh, I faced Gino. "I'm sorry."

He caressed my cheek with his knuckles. "We will pick up where we left off." Then he kissed me soft and quick on the lips.

Good grief, my Italian witch was hot.

CHAPTER NINE

My time with Gino left me feeling unsatisfied and hopeful. Not exactly the best frame of mind to spar. But Phenex was right. We had to connect without our elemental powers or we'd never get them back. How else did we have any hope of defeating Trinity and restoring our power to their rightful places if we couldn't connect any other way?

"Gino, we'll talk later, okay?" I smiled at him, glad we'd taken the time to connect. "Maybe you'd be okay with staying with me, Harper, and Noah tonight. I'd like for them to get to know you better, too."

My newest mate flashed me a wide grin. "That's

been awkward so far. Harper never did like me hanging around Elijah either."

"She's not going to have much choice in the matter now," I said with a laugh. "Mates aren't exactly something you can ignore."

He nodded. "Yeah. I'll go fill in my parents." He walked away with an expression on his face that let me know he had no real desire to tell his parents anything.

Meda waited for me in the lobby. "You okay?" she asked as Tala exited the elevator.

"Yeah. We talked, and we're going to do what we can to work it out. What else can we do?" I shrugged.

"Gino?" Tala asked.

Nodding, I turned toward the door.

"He seems like a cocky ass," she said bluntly.

Tala had always been the most abrasive of us. She'd always been the one to say the wrong thing at the wrong time, in the wrong way. Usually, I could forgive her, given her empath problem. She couldn't handle all those emotions, so she blocked them off.

Unfortunately, all too often, it made her a total bitch. "Tala, you don't know him at all."

She raised her eyebrows at me as we pushed the tinted glass doors open and walked out into the breezy afternoon air. "What's to know? You can't say he's not cocky."

"I *can* say that." I jutted out my chin. "Where are we doing this?"

Meda pointed toward the other side of the board-walk. "Phenex told me to meet him down the beach. Away from everyone." We nodded at people we'd known all our lives, people Meda would one day rule. Waving at kids and acquaintances, we walked quickly so nobody would try to stop us and talk. We'd learned that trick early on. Wave and look busy.

A cat darted across the boardwalk in front of us with a tiny vampire chasing after it.

I felt the moment my sisters realized we'd forgotten Marvin. Because my stomach dropped at the same moment. "Marvin," we gasped in unison.

I clapped my hand over my mouth.

Tala scrunched her eyes shut. "How could we forget Marvin?"

Tears sprang to Meda's eyes. She'd bonded with him more than Tala or me. "We have to go back for him."

Phenex interrupted us as we stepped onto the sand. "Go back for who?"

I hadn't realized he was behind us and his voice made me jump out of my skin.

"Marvin," Meda said. "Our cat."

"Ah, yes. The furball. I'm sure he's perfectly fine." Phenex didn't sound worried. "Does he have access to the outdoors?"

"No, he's an inside cat," I murmured. "He'll have enough dry food in his bowl for the day, but then he'd have nothing to eat." I looked up at him with big eyes. "He'll starve."

Meda and Tala stopped and turned to face Phenex. The three of us knew exactly what we were doing. We'd done it so many times over the years to our *niswi* that it had become like second nature.

Big eyes, puffy lips, innocent expressions.

It worked on our mates as easily as it did our parents.

Well, not our mom. It never worked on her. She just rolled her eyes. We'd learned early not to bother with her. She saw reason and facts, not pitiful expressions.

"I'll go get him. Tonight, after your practice." We gave him a triple-watt smile, all of us relieved to hear he'd go get our sweet kitty. It wasn't easy, all three of us hugging him at the same time, but we managed it. He practically purred with the contact.

"Okay, okay." He laughed and disentangled himself from our clutches. "Come on. We need to go down the beach until we're well separated from the crowd, then try to get you girls some power flowing."

As we started down the beach, I had to stop and slip off my sandals, letting my toes sink into the warm sand. The warm wind off the water lifted my hair, teasing me and mocking the fact that I couldn't harness it.

I felt so heavy since I lost my air. Before, my body was light, limber. The expression 'floating on air' was literal for me.

Not now. The earth had a grip on me, holding me close like she'd never let me feel the rush of my element.

When Phenex thought he'd gone far enough, he stopped and faced us. "You have the power and energy of every living thing around you. Plus, you can connect to your inherent power from Hell. Not to mention the power each of you was born with, which is not a small amount."

Harper and Noah moved closer to me, I felt them in the back of my mind, growing slowly closer. I knew they couldn't let me be away from them for long. Though, now that I thought about it, they probably thought I was this far away with Gino. Whoops.

Reaching out to them, I tried to reassure them, but Tala interrupted me. "Ami, why don't you try connecting with Hell?" She put one hand on her hip. "Maybe if you'd been able to when Trinity came, we wouldn't be in this mess."

"Is it my fault it was closed off to me? How could you blame me?" No way that was my fault. Just because they were born before me, didn't give either of them the right to think they were any better than me. Sure, they sparred more, but Meda was better at that than Tala. Neither of them were as good at their studies as I was, and like Tala said before, I'd likely do better with the magic than either of them. They were too into the physical side of our gifts.

Tala opened her mouth, and by the expression on her face, she wasn't going to say anything nice.

"No, but if we'd had time to practice this, maybe it wouldn't have ended the way it did," Meda said, cutting Tala off.

"Well, it did. And I didn't see either of you lifting a finger to stop her from doing it," I said, more acid in my tone than I'd intended.

"Ladies," Phenex said. "We are in an extremely high-tension situation. The last thing you three need to do is turn on one another."

He was right. I sighed, looking at Tala. "He's right."

She bristled, and I knew whatever was going to come out of her mouth, it wouldn't be an apology. "It doesn't make it less true. Why don't you try to connect to hell?" She tossed her hair in a very Tala fashion. Only she could make a head movement look sarcastic. "See if you can do it now."

"Fine," I said through gritted teeth as Harper and Noah moved ever closer. They were going pretty fast. I wasn't sure if they felt my anger and unsteady emotions, or they just didn't trust Gino to have me so far away from them.

I ignored them and focused on the part of me that was connected to Poppy. It helped me find the connection to Hell, and try to tap into those powers.

They opened up to me with ease this time. "Maybe Trinity managed to block my connection somehow," I said. "When she got our powers."

The power flowed into me, and as Meda and Tala connected to me, it moved through me into them.

"Or maybe you struggled to perform under pressure," Tala said under her breath.

I let go of the power abruptly, yanking it out of my sisters in the process. The sudden loss of the magic left them both reeling. "What the fuck, Ami?" Tala said.

"Ami, I know she's being especially crude today," Meda said in a bossy tone. "But that's no reason to drop the magic like that. It hurt."

She rubbed at her chest as she lectured.

"I'm struggling," I said. "I *was* struggling with the loss of my air, but at the moment it's with being gracious toward the two of you." My normally sweet and kind voice came out waspish. I didn't like it.

"Me?" Meda asked in outrage. "What did I do?"

"Boss, boss, boss," Tala said, then blew a raspberry. "You were born first, do you have to remind us of it every second of every day?"

Meda's jaw dropped, but before she could retaliate, Tala turned to me. "And you. Grow a damn backbone once in a while, would you? God. There's more to life than what's in a book."

Narrowing my eyes on her, I opened the connection to Hell again, but only a minuscule amount. Grabbing a thread of Hell power, I used it to whip at Tala, essentially slapping her in the face with it.

She stumbled backward with a gasp. "Ami," she hissed. "How dare you?"

"You're the one that wanted backbone! Deal with it."

She moved her hands as if to command her water to do her bidding, but of course, it didn't come. Her face reddened and the next thing I knew, my head snapped back as I was hit by a...something, right in the nose.

Squealing, I opened the flow of power more, ready to knock her on her sarcastic ass.

"Enough," Phenex thundered. I cut off the flow of power and looked at him, panting. "What is wrong with the three of you?"

I looked at my sisters, but my anger wouldn't dissipate. With a growl, I whirled and stalked down the beach in the direction we'd come.

I spotted Harper and Noah, running full speed toward me, but I didn't stop or even slow when they reached me. As soon as my sisters were out of sight, I yanked my shorts and tee off, stripping down to my lacy pink bra and panties. Then I walked into the ocean, ignoring Harper and Noah's calls. I heard Noah sigh. "Rock, paper, scissors for who goes after her?" he asked.

I kept going. They could come or not. A few laps in the warm, salty water might help calm me down. If not, I'd find Tala and slap her for real.

CHAPTER TEN

I floated on the water and tried to pretend it was my air flowing around me, holding me up. What the hell was wrong with us? Sure, we fight as all sisters do, but we'd never gone at each other like that. Not with that level of venom.

And I was still pissed that they turned on me, blaming me for not connecting to Hell. They had the ability to do so as much as I did. Why couldn't they tap into it?

I sensed Noah moments before he reached out and touched my hand. I lowered myself to tread water, but he pulled me to him, hugging me close. "I've never felt so much anger from you. It was like it wasn't you at all. Too much darkness."

I pulled back and studied his features. He was

right. "Do you think it might be the same curse that's blocking our elements causing a mood shift?"

He shrugged. "It's possible. I'm not familiar with curses and magic. All I know is Harper and I felt it, and it was dark. Like it was fueling your anger. And it would be something Trinity would do to keep you and your sisters from combining your powers."

That was plausible. And very much something Trinity would do to weaken us. A very small part of me wanted to rush off and tell Meda and Tala about Noah's theory. But the larger part didn't want to see them anytime soon. Tala had said some hurtful things. I got angrier thinking about it.

"I'll talk to my sisters and Phenex later. I don't want to see them right now." I leaned my head back into the water until it covered my ears. I could totally see why Tala liked to drown in her water. Too bad I couldn't drown in my air right now.

Noah traced a finger down my throat and into my cleavage. "Let's go up to our room so Harper and I can make you feel better."

Dirty thoughts entered my mind, making me smile. That sounded like the perfect distraction at the moment. "That sounds amazing. But afterward, we need to talk about Gino."

Noah let out a soft growl as he swam beside me.

"I figured we'd have to soon. Harper doesn't trust him. It was all I could do to keep her from stalking the two of you."

When I emerged from the water, I saw Harper on shore with a large, fluffy beach towel. I walked into it, and she wrapped it around me, hugging me to her and kissing my cheek. "Feel better?"

"Not really, but I will."

Noah collected my clothes and sandals before following Harper and me to the hotel. Relief flooded my system when we entered the large penthouse apartment and the common area was empty. Even though I was a little calmer, I still didn't want to face my sisters.

After a quick shower, I dressed in my favorite babydoll nightie and a pair of sexy black panties. When I entered the room I shared with my two mates, I found them stretched out on one of the large beds, Harper flipping through TV channels.

Glancing at me, Harper's sensual lips lifted in a smile, and she turned off the television and tossed the remote onto the end table. "I don't know why you bothered with putting on clothes."

My lips lifted and so did my desires. "I know how you like a challenge."

"And ripping your clothes off you." Desire

whipped through her blue eyes, sending a shudder through me, and I groaned at the hunger in her gaze.

Noah moved to the other bed with a grin. "You two don't mind me."

Harper gave him a narrowed-eyed gaze before she focused back on me. "He's a perv."

"Yeah, but he's our perv."

Her smile turned wicked as she stalked closer. After the mess on the beach with my sisters, I needed something else to focus on. And my mates were the perfect distraction. The idea of having both of them at the same time sent a shockwave of desire rolling through me. With a low growl, I pushed Harper on to the bed.

She laughed but also didn't take her eyes off of me as I climbed on the bed, hovering over her. "You still have your clothes on." I leaned down and pressed a soft kiss on her lips.

"Damn." Noah hissed. "Watching isn't enough, not by a long shot." By the sounds, he had gotten off the bed. The rustling of clothes told me he was stripping down. Harper, however, locked gazes with me, challenging me. "Why don't you take care of that?"

My insides lit up like fireworks. A low growl rumbled out of me as I ripped her shirt off, then yanked down her pants. I stared at her creamy, smooth skin, beckoning me to caress every inch of her. Leaning down, I pressed a kiss to her belly, then nipped my way down to the top of her panties.

Growling, I ripped them off by taking them between my teeth, then yanking down, then returning my gaze to her face to see her reaction. Her eyes flashed with her inner vampire and her fangs lengthened. As much as I wanted to tease her, I needed to taste her. I pressed a kiss to her thigh, then spread her legs to cover her core with my mouth. Harper sucked in a breath and then groaned as I flicked my tongue over her clit. She tasted like the ocean, a little salty, and a little metallic. Every time I tasted her, it was a little different, depending on what she'd eaten, how much blood she'd consumed, and how turned on she was. Her creamy folds told me she was extremely turned on today.

Harper threaded her hands in my hair and rotated her hips, grinding against my mouth as I sucked and nipped, then pressed my face against her to push my tongue as far inside as it would reach. She liked it, because her hips bucked. I did it again for good measure.

Noah crawled on the bed behind me and slipped my black panties down my hips, then gripped my ass cheeks. I lifted them, giving him complete access. He cupped me and slid two fingers through my folds. My body jerked under his touch and pleasure started to build almost instantly. When he slipped those fingers inside me, I gasped. Hot liquid desire filled me as he pumped his fingers in and out, curling them in the perfect direction.

As an orgasm built inside me, thanks to Noah's skilled hands, I sucked harder on Harper's clit and entered her with two fingers, twisting them as I pumped in and out. Noah found a rhythm, and I matched it inside Harper. She reached down, spreading her lips apart to give me better access to her clit as she moaned.

Noah withdrew his fingers, and I held in a whimper. When he teased my entrance with his cock, my body heated, ready to feel him inside me, but he pushed inside far too slowly. "Noah, I don't need slow right now." I thrust back toward him, sinking a bit farther onto his cock.

He chuckled and sank inside me, filling me completely. I cried out and pressed back into him while increasing the pressure of my fingers inside Harper. The stretch of my vaginal walls around Noah's considerable cock gave me an intense feeling, heightening the pleasure. Noah moved fast and hard, as he knew I preferred it.

My favorite part of being bonded to my mates was the shared pleasure when we had sex or touched one another. I knew that Harper's pleasure was doubled by mine. Just my pleasure was tripled. I felt Noah's and Harper's on top of my own. An orgasm with Gino hopefully added to the mix one day would be phenomenal.

"Fuck," Noah growled out as he slammed into me over and over. The sound of our skin slapping together filled the air. I watched Harper's face. She opened her eyes and twisted her neck, watching Noah fuck me. I grinned. So, she had all the big words about Noah watching, but the minx wanted to see his cock going in and out of me. I considered how I'd feel watching Noah sink himself into Harper, and the idea nearly took my orgasm over the edge.

I moved my mouth to Harper's thigh and sank my fangs into her skin. She screamed out in pleasure, her strong orgasm making her body buck under me. I held her down, thankful for my strength, and nearly lost myself. The feel of Noah's cock slamming into me fought for my full attention against the sounds of our sex: slapping skin, Noah's grunts, my moans, and Harp's screams. Harper's orgasm was particularly strong, and I wanted to keep it going, so I tried to focus on fucking her with my hand as my fangs drew out her sweet, delicious blood. My orgasm tore through me moments later, shifting my attention to it. My inner walls trembled as Noah escalated, his climax making him move even faster and harder. As a lycan, he was able to go pretty damn hard. My body slammed against Harper, even though I'd pulled my fingers out. I lowered my mouth to her core since she still squirmed underneath me. As Noah finished, and my body jerked into hers, my mouth moved over her clit without much effort on my part, so I could enjoy the last gusts of my orgasm.

I licked the blood that had run out of the puncture marks, then licked the holes, helping them heal. They would've healed on their own in seconds, anyway, but I wanted to taste her one more time.

Noah pulled out and rubbed his hands over my ass, following with kisses. "Can you handle more?" he asked.

I sat up and looked at him in surprise. I'd thought he'd orgasmed, but his dick was as hard as ever.

Looking down at Harper, still lying on the bed panting as her orgasm waned, I thought about her interest in watching Noah fuck me. Would I enjoy watching him fuck her?

"Harp," I said cautiously. "Have you ever had sex with a man?"

She looked from Noah to me and shook her head. "Only you, Ami."

"Okay," I said, leaning down and pressing a kiss to her lips. "Never mind." We had a strap-on hidden in our bedroom in the dorm, so I knew for sure she'd been penetrated, but the picture of the two of them joining, with me there, touching, watching. Now I was the perv.

"What?" Harper asked, eyeing Noah's dick. It was bigger than the strap-on we used. "Were you thinking about him fucking me?"

I bit my lip and nodded. "I know you're not into guys. But we've gotten so close. And..." I chewed on my lip and felt foolish. "I'm not asking. Forget it. I'd never want to do anything that made you feel uncomfortable."

Noah sat through the whole thing with wide eyes, purposefully not looking at Harper's pussy, still on display. She'd never closed her legs. I wasn't sure if he realized it, but his hand was on his dick, stroking.

Harper studied my face, then her eyes returned to Noah. "Let's say I'm mildly intrigued."

I grinned. She wanted to do it! She was curious. I probed her bond and found her so turned on it made my core pulse. "You want to know what it feels like?" I asked.

She nodded.

I looked back at Noah. He looked like the cat that ate the canary. "Ami, I'm in love with you. You know that, right?"

Knee walking to him, I grabbed his face and pulled him close. "I love you too. So much. You're funny and protective and know when to not be too protective. You're constantly there for me, and give me amazing orgasms."

He smiled. "Please don't ask me to name everything I love about you. We'd be here all night because my mind goes blank when I'm with you. All I see or hear is you."

"Nice," Harper said. "I feel that way, too." Looking back, I saw she had one hand on her breasts, teasing her nipples, and the other between her legs, teasing her clit.

"You two are really turned on," I said as I felt their desire through the bond.

"Yeah, but just because I'm curious what sex with a man feels like, doesn't mean I love you any less. I'll be perfectly content with your sweet cunt the rest of our lives." Harper grinned at me and spread her lips. "And you're amazing mouth."

Her opening squeezed, and I watched her inner walls clench. "I'd like to see Noah fuck that beautiful pussy," I whispered, feeling selfish. What if my desire was influencing something neither of them wanted to do?

I looked at Noah. "I'm sorry. It's too weird, isn't it?"

He shook his head. "After watching you eat her pussy, I'll never look at either of you the same again. The affectionate, friendly relationship has been altered a bit, I think. I'm not going to lie to you, I'm attracted to her. And I love her. But I'm *in* love with you, to the bottom of my soul."

I was good with that. Settling on my side beside Harper, my head near her navel, I ran my hands through her slick core. "You're sure?" I asked, looking at both of them.

"Can I have a safe word? I'm afraid it will hurt, or I'll hate it."

"Of course," Noah and I exclaimed at the same time.

"Whatever you want it to be," I said.

"Okay. How about goddess?" She grinned. "Because you two are making me feel like one."

"Perfect." I reached out my hand, slick from her

juices, and grabbed Noah's cock. If possible, he was harder than before. "You ready?"

He moved forward, dropping onto his hands and knees.

"Pull your knees up," I whispered, then pressed a kiss to Harper's stomach. She did, and I repositioned myself to halfway lay over her knee.

"Come on," I coaxed Noah. Guiding his cock to her core, I rubbed his head in her wetness. She breathed hard, holding her upper body up with her hands on her knees.

Stopping his head at her entrance, I rubbed around, spreading the wetness over his head and the top part of his shaft so he'd glide into her easier.

Her eyes widened as he pressed forward. He had one arm threaded between us, and I was pressed tightly against it. It trembled as he moved slowly. "Shit," he hissed. "You're fucking tight."

I couldn't resist the chance to tease him. "Tighter than me?"

He grunted, and his eyes widened. Freezing in place, he looked at me. "Um."

Harper and I both laughed, and when she did, I saw her pussy tighten around the tip of his head, all he'd gotten inside her so far. He moaned and flexed his hips, which pushed him in enough for the ridges of his head to disappear.

Harper's laugh turned into a moan.

"Oh, do you like that?" I whispered, still stroking her lips and teasing her clit, then moving to squeeze Noah's shaft as he tried so hard to go slow.

"It feels so..." She searched for the right word. "Full."

I giggled as I returned my attention to her pussy. "I understand what you mean."

"I have to move," Noah said in a strained voice.

Harper shifted slightly. "Go ahead."

He inched forward, his shaft disappearing inch by inch inside her. He was gifted with length and girth, and when he hit it hard, I felt him go very deep inside me. She was feeling that now, for the first time. I envied her. It hadn't been all that long ago it was me, and it had been a delicious feeling.

When Noah was fully seated, I moved my hand to cover Harper's clit. "Fuck her," I whispered. "Make her come."

He grunted and pulled almost all the way out. I continued rubbing her clit with my fingertips, enjoying the feel of it rolling under my hand. Sliding back in, she gasped, since he went much faster this time. "Oh," she whispered.

I smiled and turned my head. Her nipple wasn't far from my mouth, so I scooted up so I could suck it between my lips.

All this playing and watching was giving me a seriously wet core. I'd need one more orgasm before it was over.

"Noah," I said in a bossy tone. "Make her come. But you can't yet."

His face blanched. "That's not going to be easy."

"I don't care how tight and hot her pussy is. You will come in me."

Nodding, he thrust forward harder than he probably meant to. Harper squealed. "That was good," she gasped. "Good yell, not bad."

She was beyond full sentences. I could help with that.

"Harder," I commanded, then pulled her nipple into my mouth again, letting my fangs sink in a fraction of an inch. Just enough to spur on the orgasm she'd have with him soon anyway.

She let out a throaty yell. "God she clamped down," Noah said, his teeth clenched. "I can't."

His hips flexed and he hung his head, watching his dick move in and out of Harper. I bit deeper and pushed my hand harder on her clit. She screamed again as Noah began moving in earnest, almost as fast and hard as he had with me. When she started to relax, I realized he was moving harder, as if winding up for his release. "Stop," I said in my most alpha voice.

He stopped, grabbed his dick, and squeezed the head after pulling fully out of Harper. I licked the bite wounds on her perfect tit and smiled at her. She nodded. "I don't know if I want to do that every time. But I'm not mad at it."

Laughing, I rolled over on my back and spread my legs.

"I'm not going to last long," Noah said with his eyes on my pussy.

"A little help?" I asked Harper.

She grinned. "Gladly." Positioning herself exactly as I'd been moments ago on her, she reached over and pressed her fingers into my clit. "Time for payback."

Noah was much faster with me. He knew he wouldn't hurt me. I lifted my legs to rest on his shoulders, and he pounded into me with an abandon he couldn't have with Harper.

An orgasm washed over me almost immediately as Harper worked my clit and Noah wore my pussy out. "I'm coming," he grunted a few minutes later. I'd already known by the speed increase, but his words were for Harper. She sank her fangs into my breast in the same spot I'd bitten her minutes before.

The orgasm broke, sending me into a vortex of pleasure. I wasn't sure whose grunts, cries, and moans belonged to who, but by the time I finished, all three of us were breathing like we'd run a marathon.

Noah gathered me in his arms and pulled us beside Harper, still inside me. We laid like that for a few minutes before Noah pulled out and shifted to press against me.

Sandwiched bonelessly between Noah and Harper, the afterglow of sex hummed through me, tingling every part of my body. I draped over Noah's chest with one leg over one of his, my hips twisted and my chest facing the ceiling. Harper cuddled up to my side with her cheek pressed to mine.

As much as I didn't want to screw up our blissful state, we had to talk about Gino. "What do you know about Gino?"

"His family is into dark magic." Harper growled.

I laughed. I couldn't help it. "Have you met my grandfather? Some people know him as Satan."

Noah laughed. "She has a point, Harper. Pick a different reason to hate him."

"I don't hate him. I just don't like him."

I turned to face her. "Why?"

She frowned. "He's secretive. I don't trust people who keep secrets."

It was my turn to frown. "So you know him well enough that he should share his secrets with you?"

"No." Harper sighed and rolled to her back. "Okay, fine, I don't know him. I judge him based off of rumors and the fact his family is the witches' version of the mob."

I fell silent and twined my fingers with hers. "He's my mate, just as you and Noah are. I can't stop it."

Harper framed my face and pulled me down until our lips brushed together. "I know. I guess I'm worried about his strong personality. Guys like him don't take no for an answer. And they're known to break women who are more alpha than they are. Force them to be submissive."

Frowning, I stared into her gaze. "I don't sense that from him. Besides, do you think I'd let him walk all over me? My personality isn't as strong as Meda's or Tala's, but I'm still an alpha female."

Noah rose up behind me and kissed my shoulder. "We worry about you. It's our job to protect you."

I rolled my eyes as a knock sounded on our door. I sensed Gino on the other side. Well, the intense need to screw his brains out, anyway. I jumped up and grabbed my nightie. "That's Gino. I invited him to come up."

Harper growled, and I shot her a look that commanded her to be nice. She held my gaze for a few moments before looking away. She was also a dominant female, but I outranked her. With a sigh, I said, "Have an open mind. And no growling. Either of you."

Noah held his hands up and smirked. "I'll play nice as long as he does."

I pursed my lips and opened the door. Gino lifted a brow, then raked his gaze over me. Desire swirled in his dark depths. He stepped into my personal space and wrapped an arm around my waist, shutting the door behind him. "You make it so hard for me to be a gentleman."

Pressing my palms to his chest, I gave a little push. It was a warning. I could overpower him if I wanted, and I could tell he knew that. He leaned into me and captured my lips in a searing, passion-filled kiss. Was he trying to stake claim on me in front of my other two mates? As much as I wanted to strip him naked and take him right there, I needed to respect Harper and Noah. I bit down on Gino's bottom lip, making him jerk away from me.

Staring at me with heat in his gaze, he smiled. "My apologies. The pull is strong."

"Tell me about it," I mumbled and stepped out of his embrace. "Gino, these are my other mates, Harper and Noah."

Noah gave him a nod as he tucked the blanket around his waist. Harper grunted and plucked Noah's shirt off the floor, pulling it over her head. A sheepish grin formed on my face. I guess I could have let them dress before opening the door. Oops.

Gino took a seat on the empty bed, his expression void of emotion. "I feel a little overdressed."

Well, he could remove some clothes. I banished that thought quickly.

An awkward silence filled the room. I didn't know what to say and my body itched to be close to him. At the same time I felt like if I moved to the bed with Gino, it would be a betrayal of my other two mates.

Finally, after a few more minutes I blurted, "How is this going to work? I mean Harper and Noah have known each other and me since they started sentry training at thirteen."

Gino nodded. "I'm not going anywhere. And I've been way more patient than I normally am."

There was a darkness to his tone that made me

shiver. Not out of fear, but desire. I opened my mouth to speak, but Harper's words cut me off. "Ami is our alpha. Her well-being and strength is for us to protect and nourish. I will not allow anyone to come in and break her."

Gino's chocolate depths darkened as he locked gazes with Harper. "My intentions are not to break her. Her strong will is what attracts me, besides the hunger of meeting a true mate." He looked at me and my insides ignited into a wildfire of need. "I'm all in. I know I have to share you with two others, and I'm willing to make the effort to make it work. Besides, if you haven't noticed from your encounter with my mother, strong-minded and strong-willed females run in my family. I still think you handled her beautifully."

I didn't like to "handle" people. That was Meda's job. However, Gino's mother was a force to be reckoned with. To my surprise, I liked the little verbal sparring match I'd had with the woman. "Did they come to the island?"

Gino shook his head. "She was quite put out that I did."

The wide smile that formed on his face after he spoke made me giggle. I could see his mom being pissed that he followed his mate to a realm she couldn't access. Especially when she thought it wasn't his fight. That last thought made me frown. "Are you sure you're ready for our upcoming fight?"

He gave a sharp nod. "You're my mate, Ami. I'll do what I need to in order to protect you and your family and your people."

I glanced at Harper and saw her press her lips into a thin line. Then she sent me a thought through our bond. *I guess he can stay.*

Smiling, I puckered my lips at her. *Thank you for trying.*

She poked my ribs making me jump. *If he hurts you, I'll kill him.*

We spent the next several hours talking, watching movies, and playing games. The tension about the pending battle was high and it was nice to spend a night being normal. Plus, it allowed all three of my mates to get to know each other better. It gave me hope that the relationship would work. I needed to take some time to spend with each of them. But we'd figure that all out after we dealt with Trinity.

It was about two a.m. when Noah got up and dressed in his dark gray sentry uniform. Well, unofficial uniform that Mom suggested the sentries wear. Noah and Harper said they were comfortable and liked wearing them. After dressing, he pressed a lingering kiss to my lips. "I'm on post. Randall doesn't trust that Trinity can't breach the portals."

Nodding, I said. "See you soon."

He winked at me, then met Harper's gaze briefly before bending down like he was going to kiss her. She placed her palm on his face and pushed him away. "Don't make me kick your ass."

Noah laughed, nodded to Gino, and left our room.

A few minutes later, Gino put his shoes on and stood. He kissed my forehead. "I'll see you tomorrow."

Harper grabbed me by the waist and pulled me on down to lay beside her. "We're having a meeting late morning. You're welcome to attend."

Gino glanced at her with a hint of surprise, then nodded. "Thank you."

When Gino left, Harper kissed my neck. "Now I have you all to myself."

I giggled and removed my nightie. "As do I."

Desire lit up her gaze and her fangs poked out from her lips. For the love of all unholy, I loved this woman.

CHAPTER ELEVEN

"Ami." Harper's voice broke through my deep sleep.

"What?" I whispered. It had to be the middle of the night. My scratchy eyes didn't want to open.

"Wake up," she whispered. Light fingers danced down my bare spine. "It's getting late."

"What are you talking about?" I asked groggily. "We *just* went to sleep."

"Hey," Harper said more urgently. "Are you okay?"

I cracked an eye at her. "Sure, why?"

"You're always up before everyone else, usually with your nose stuck in a book. I know we're in a high intensity situation, but I would've thought you'd at least want to check out the cool stuff your Poppy provided."

She made a valid point, but why would I want to do that stuff in the middle of the night? "Harp, we can do all that in the morning."

I rolled over to try to go back to sleep and wished Noah was still in bed with me.

"Ami. Seriously. Look around. The sun is shining bright through the window. I'm not sure what's up with time in this place, but it seems to flow just like home, because according to my watch, it's after noon, and according to the sun in the sky, my watch is accurate."

After noon? No way. "That's not possible." I sat up and rubbed my eyes, then looked out of the windows that gave a gorgeous view of the ocean. The sun was high in the sky, all right. "Damn."

Harper's face looked pinched and worried.

"Oh, calm down, I was probably just tired," I said through a yawn. "It's all good."

"I know, I'm just making sure you're okay after the stressful day you had yesterday."

Her concern bordered on irritating. "Harper. Will you chill?"

"Sure," she said in a quiet voice. "I'll leave you alone to get ready."

Her hurt pulsed through the bond. Part of me wanted to call out to her and ask her to come back in, but I didn't. She'd get over it, and I needed a breather, time away from those two.

At least they'd given me a great orgasm the night before.

What's wrong with you? You're never so callous.

Great. I was beginning to annoy myself.

After dressing, I stepped out of my bedroom into the hotel room common area to find Meda with her fist raised, about to knock on my door. "Is Phenex in there?" she demanded.

"No." I pushed past her toward the coffee maker.

"I can't find him anywhere."

While I measured out coffee to make a fresh pot, I reached internally for his bond.

It wasn't there. Or, it was, but it was muted, like someone had laid a thick blanket over it. What the hell?

"Where is he?" I asked as I poured water into the reservoir.

"The last I spoke to him, he was going to pop in and get Marvin," she said in a scared tone. "What if that went wrong?"

Rounding on her, I narrowed my eyes. "You let him go *alone?*"

"Why wouldn't I? He can make tiny little portals to spy and make sure nothing bad could get him. He's not stupid."

It was increasingly difficult to keep my temper. "Yeah, but what if Marvin wouldn't come to him? And he was exposed long enough for Trinity to realize he was there?" My fearless leader obviously hadn't thought of that.

Her face paled. "We've got to get to him."

My parents and Tala walked in the door as Meda covered her face with her hands.

"What's going on?" our mom asked. "Why is she crying?"

"I have no idea," I said. "She's missing Phenex for five minutes and she acts like it's the end of the world."

Mom shot me a surprised expression. "Meda rarely cries, Ami, you know that. If she's driven to tears, the threat must be sincere. And since when are you so cynical?"

"Yeah, like she can focus long enough to be cynical," Tala muttered.

"That's it," I yelled. "Outside, now. You're being a bitch."

"I'm always a bitch," Tala countered. "What's your excuse?"

"Enough," Dad yelled. Meda looked up from her sob-fest, and Tala and I turned toward him. "Something is going on with you three. You've never been so out of sync."

"I think it's their curse," Noah said. I hadn't even realized he was out in the hallway. My parents hadn't made it all the way in the door, so we couldn't see that most of our mates and sentries were behind them, heading in.

Everyone moved farther into the room, filling it quickly. I sighed as I looked at the enormous crowd. Even Gino was with them. "What's this?"

"We figured out Phenex was missing hours ago," Harper said. "But you three slept through our search."

Tala held her hands up. "I helped you search."

"Moving from the bedroom to the hammock hardly counts as helping us search," Randell said, face serious. She just shrugged.

Sterling sat in the middle of the floor, followed by Gino and Fenton. "One thing we all agree about is that you are acting completely out of character."

Gino winked at me. "Come on over here, mate."

I sighed and walked over, more interested in the way his shaggy black hair curled around his ears than what he wanted to do with his magic. I wondered if I could come up with a sneaky way to get us out of here so we could finally complete the whole mated thing.

"None of that now," he said, picking up my mood. "We've got work to do."

Meda and Tala sat down in front of their witches.

Fenton, ever the teacher, stood. "Now, the mates have been talking. It's no coincidence that you each have a witch. We figure there's some sort of connection we are supposed to help you achieve. So, let's sit here and have a moment with each other. Let us do the legwork for now."

Sterling nodded. "We want to poke around in your brains for a few minutes. Are you okay with that?"

I looked at my sisters, intensely missing my connection to them. "Yeah," I said. "It's okay with me."

They nodded, both looking lost and sad. I couldn't feel that, and normally I could. "You're right," Meda said.

I finished her thought. Even without our normal connection, I knew exactly what she wanted to say. "Something is blocking us, keeping us from each other."

"Relax," Gino said. "Close your eyes." He took my hands and scooted forward until we sat knee to knee with our legs crossed.

Exhaling as much air as I could, I sucked in a deep, clean breath and focused on his voice. His sexy, sultry voice. *Darn it.* I squirmed.

He shushed me, running his thumb lightly across the back of my knuckles. The next thing I knew, the six of us were lost in a sea of murky black. "This is what's causing your anger," Gino said.

I looked around, but as soon as I looked away from his face, I nearly lost myself in the darkness. "I can't stand this," I whispered.

"Then get rid of it."

I focused on the blackness, willing it to leave, but nothing happened. "I feel like Meda could burn it off if she had her flames."

"That's the point though, isn't it? This is keeping you from your elements."

I centered myself and drew on energy from my family in the room near me. Gino and I were lost in my head, but physically they were nearby.

It worked. The essence of my *niswi*, Harper and Noah flooded into me. I didn't draw from Mom, just in case it put too much strain on the baby. Once again, I willed the black murk away, but it was to no avail.

"Try Hell," Gino suggested. "Or we could try you funneling your power to me. I can try to get rid of it."

Hell was being difficult so I tried his other idea. "Okay, sure," I said. Focusing on Gino, I pushed the power I'd pulled from my family at my mate. He yelled and disappeared from my mind. I opened my eyes, jerking myself out of the trance with a gasp. "Are you okay?"

He pinched the bridge of his nose. "Yeah, but holy fuck."

My sisters, Fenton, and Sterling blinked and looked at us. "What happened?" Meda asked.

"She tried to let me take control of her power, to see if I could push the black crap away, but when I tried, it was far more power than I could ever handle." He looked at me with a shocked expression. "I knew you triplets were powerful, but damn."

"I was afraid this might happen," Sterling said. "Meda is too powerful for me to help, I think. I'm not sure what the purpose was, them having the three of us. I'm sure there's a point, but I haven't seen it yet."

"So, we're on our own. Again," Tala said.

"That's not so bad." I tried to keep an eye on the blackness, and contain it in my mind. If I sequestered it, I felt more like myself. "Put the curse in a box. Lock it up tight."

Tala narrowed her eyes at me, but then she closed them. In a moment she breathed in sharply. "That makes a difference."

"We may not be able to remove it, but if we can ignore it, maybe we can get through this," I said. I still couldn't reach my air, but I definitely breathed easier.

Meda laughed. "It does feel much better."

"Finally," Mom muttered. "Okay, girls, you sit here until you figure out how to make a portal. We've got to get that damn hound back."

That was easier said than done. We connected to each other, pulled power back and forth between us. We brought our mates in, and while we didn't give them our power to harness, we figured out how to sidle them up to us so that we could harness it together. We couldn't make it work with each other though. It seemed we could connect to our mates or each other, but not both.

When that novelty ran its course, we tried connecting to Hell.

That's when the real magic started. With the power of Hell running through us, we were able to connect to each other and our mates. I felt Fenton and Sterling through my sisters, and they could feel Gino. "Now we're getting somewhere," Gino said, and held out his hand. He made a flower appear, bloom, then wilt and die, then reversed it. Then he conjured a necklace with an enormous emerald.

"Gino Drago, you put that back around the rich lady's neck you took it from," I scolded him.

It wasn't around her neck. It was locked in the Tower of London.

I gasped and looked at him with wide eyes. *You can't go around stealing the Crown Jewels, Gino!*

His eyes sparkled. "You're a princess, are you not?"

I studied the necklace. What other occasion would I have to see such a thing close up? "Can you send it back?"

"Of course," he said. "With this power, I could duplicate it."

I looked around the room at my family. They didn't look happy. "Would that be so bad?" I asked.

My mother nodded. "If that's what I think it is, yes. That would be bad."

"Okay," he said, and the necklace disappeared. "Back to a portal."

I focused on my bedroom in our dorm. I'd once read a book that said reality was made up of fabric, woven in time, space, and reality. In that vein, I plucked mentally at the wall separating me from the room in my mind.

To my amazement, it moved. "Guys," I whispered as I grasped another thread. "Hey," I hissed.

I felt more than saw them move closer to me. "It's working," I said with a nervous laugh as I continued plucking at the threads. "It's like unraveling a tapestry."

"Can you cut it instead of unraveling it?" Meda asked.

I tried, reaching out with my magic to slice a hole in the tapestry instead of picking at it.

"Yes," I crowed. "It's working."

"We can see that," my mom said. "I can see the inside of your bedroom. She stood behind me, judging by the location of her voice. "Great job, darling."

CHAPTER TWELVE

I sliced into the tapestry, making the hole between the two realms bigger until it was large enough we could walk through. "I don't think we should all go through," I said, peering into my bedroom. Nothing looked out of place, but that didn't guarantee anything.

Meda nodded. "In case Trinity is lurking around, Tala, Ami and I can get in and out a lot quieter."

Randell growled, not liking the idea. "I'm going."

Tala rolled her eyes but when she opened her mouth to tell him he wasn't, Dorian and Harper stood and said at the same time, "We're going too."

The *niswi* glowered. "If you're not back in three minutes, we're coming through."

"Fine, whatever. Dorian, you can stand in the

doorway and keep the people on the other side of the portal updated," Meda said and faced the portal. It was easier to humor them. "Ready?"

After Tala and I nodded, we walked through and into my room at the dorm. Meda moved to the door and listened. "Someone is moving around."

"Smells like demons," Tala added in a flat tone. "Several."

We met each other's gazes and took a breath at the same time. Meda said, "We have to fight the darkness and work together. Marvin and Phenex are depending on us."

Nodding, I opened myself to the power of Hell. It came quickly this time. "I'm ready."

A glance at our mates behind us told us they were ready as well. Meda twisted the knob and threw the door open. The sight in the common area froze us in our tracks. Phenex slouched over, held upright by the ropes tying him to the kitchen chair. It looked like he'd been beaten pretty badly. My heart splintered seeing him injured and broken. It also pissed me off. Phenex was mine and my sisters. No one hurt our mate.

A fierce growl ripped from me as I charged forward. I may not have been as strong of a fighter as my sisters, but I still trained with Randell, who never went easy on me. Plus, these bastard demons hurt my Phenex. They were going to pay for it.

Fueled by my rage and protectiveness for my hound, I slammed into a demon close to Phenex, slashing at him with my hand. My claws sliced into his skin with ease. What? My claws? When the heck did I learn to partially shift? I knew mom could shift at will, but this was different. Mom was the first High Alpha to do so in centuries. The demon retaliated while I stared in amazement at my claw-hands. Jumping back, I blocked his kick and moved past the amazement of my discover. No time to think too much about it at the moment, but I'd sure use it to my advantage.

The demon screamed and jumped back when I slashed him again. Then he snarled at me and charged. I bumped into Harper at my back, battling her own demon as I focused on pulling the power of Hell into me. Splitting my focus between fighting the bleeding demon and directing the magic took everything I had. I rounded a kick to his gut, sending him flying into the far wall.

When my chi filled with power, I pushed it out to my sisters, keeping an equal amount for myself. After forming a ball of energy, I threw it at another demon as he turned his attention to me. the energy ball hit him in the chest, vanquishing him.

A demon screech to my right drew my attention. Tala hit it with a power ball.

"Tala. Half shift."

She glanced at me like I was delusional. Then her eyes grew round when I showed her my hands, now in claws. She glanced down at her own and in seconds they shifted. "Fucking cool. Meda!"

A growl grabbed my attention, and I whirled around to come face to face with two large demons. I pulled power from Hell and let it flow down my arms to my claws, then ran toward them. Right before I reached them, I jumped and swiped my claws across the chest of one, then pivoted to slice the other's throat. Instead of spurting, blood oozed from the wounds, and I pushed aside the bile that rose up within me.

The dark magic from Hell transferred from my claws into the demons when I struck them. It didn't take long for the oozing, wounded beasts to disinte-grate and return to Hell.

Everything fell quiet, and I glanced around to see the demons were gone. I rushed to Phenex and dropped to my knees beside him. My heart ached at the sight of the bruises on his face. Carefully, I touched his cheek. He began to stir as my sisters fell to their knees around our mate. His eyes fluttered open, then his brows dipped. "Trap. They were waiting."

"Shh," I cooed and stroked his cheek. "It's okay."

Randell checked out the rest of the dorm, most likely searching for Marvin. No matter what the grumpy sentry said, we all knew he loved that cat.

Meda choked on a sob. "Phenex." She ran her hands over his head and then his chest and stomach. Being a fire elemental, she had a small amount of healing power. Unfortunately, she couldn't turn the healing power on herself, which was the case for most healers. "He may have a few broken ribs and a lot of internal bruising. I can't soothe his pain without my fire." She banged her fists on her knees in frustration. "Damn it." Dorian walked forward and put his arms around her.

Harper put her hand on my back. "We should go," she whispered.

Tala nodded. She'd heard my mate. "We need to get him back to the island. I'm sure Trinity will come looking for her demons soon." Tala linked her fingers with Phenex's.

Randell came back from Meda's room holding Marvin. "Found him under Meda's bed. He's scared."

Meda took Marvin and nuzzled his fur while she hugged him close. "You trouble maker."

Randell placed a hand on Phenex's shoulder and bent down. "Can you walk?"

Phenex nodded, but when he tried to stand, his legs shook, and he fell back into the chair. Randell gave a half frown and scooped Phenex up with one hand supporting his back and the other under his knees so as not to jolt the hound too much.

My heart swelled to see Tala's mate treating Phenex so delicately. Maybe this whole meshed family would work. Eventually.

We shuffled back into my bedroom, but the portal was gone. Shoot. Using all my focus to fight and use magic had let the portal collapse.

Once everyone was ready, I focused on the common area in the hotel and reached out to Mom and the *niswi*. Connecting to them made it easier to form the portal back to the island.

To my relief, our parents had the shaman, Adam, there and ready to look at Phenex. Randell carried Phenex to Tala's room. My sisters and I followed on his heels. We stood to the side with our hands locked together, worry bouncing between us as we waited for the shaman to check Phenex's injuries.

It felt like hours before Adam stepped away from

Phenex's resting form. He turned to us. "He needs rest. Whoever did this weakened him with silver before beating him. I healed the minor things—bruising and fractures. The rest will be up to his natural healing abilities."

Meda nodded. "Thank you."

Adam took each of our hands and smiled. "He needs his mates right now. Just be sure not to jostle him too much."

Then he left.

Without a word to each other, we crawled on the bed with Phenex. It was a good thing the room had a king-size bed. I curled up next to him with my head on his stomach. Meda laid at my back so her head rested on the pillow beside his. Tala spooned his other side.

I laid awake listening to Meda drift off to sleep. Then Tala wasn't far behind her. When I closed my eyes, Phenex tightened his arms around me and I felt his fingers playing with the ends of my hair. "Goodnight, my mates."

Soon after, his breathing became steady as he fell asleep. I could sense through our bond that he was more relaxed.

"Goodnight, mate." I closed my eyes and let sleep take me.

CHAPTER THIRTEEN

Wy sisters and Phenex slept soundly, but I tossed and turned until I had to get up. My mind wouldn't settle. Looking down at my sisters, I smiled, but my sadness wouldn't relent. They looked content and peaceful wrapped around Phenex. Why couldn't I find that myself?

The empty common area beckoned me. I rummaged in the fridge, finding milk. A short hunt in the cabinets rewarded me with cookies.

Thanks, Poppy. He couldn't have known which set of rooms we'd claim as our own, but somehow my favorite cookies were plentiful in the cabinet.

Dragging a chair over to the gigantic window, I curled up and watched the moon dance over the water in the distance. The cookies hit the spot, and when I finished my milk, I set the rest of the cookies down with the glass on the floor beside the chair.

"Hey, Puss," I crooned as Marvin stretched and climbed into the chair with me. He settled down between my legs and the arm of the chair.

I traced my fingers along his ears, scratching and rubbing absentmindedly. My thoughts bounced from subject to subject. Gino, Trinity, the library of books, Marvin, Phenex, my air.

"Ami," Harper whispered. "Come on."

Blinking sleepily, I looked up at my mate. "I didn't mean to fall asleep," I whispered.

She bent over me, the sunrise making a halo of her blonde hair. "It's okay. I just got in from guard duty. Come lay down with me for a while."

Marvin purred at me as I stood, but he didn't follow, instead opting to curl up in the warm spot I left.

Harper took my hand, leading me to the room we were sharing with Noah while staying on the island. Technically Gino should be there as well. Maybe we could work things out so that he could join us soon. It didn't feel right, knowing he wasn't with me.

My eyes closed as soon as my head hit the pillow, and I didn't wake again until the sun beat through the windows, warming the room.

Harper grunted as I stretched. "Can't I stay and sleep?" she said through a yawn. "I hate night guard duty."

Leaning over, I pressed a firm kiss on her forehead. "Sleep. I think we're going to try to combine powers again, see if we can make some headway with this curse."

She didn't respond, already too far asleep to hear me.

After a shower, I walked into the living area to find my sisters sitting around the table. A plate piled with sandwiches sat between them.

"Where'd that come from?" I asked. My middle-of-the-night snack search hadn't turned up any sandwich fixings. I glanced over to see someone had cleaned up my cookie mess. It wasn't like me to leave it.

"The kitchens are well-stocked downstairs," Meda said around a mouthful of sandwich. She'd always been a big eater.

I couldn't remember when I'd had more than a nibble here and there. The cookies in the night hadn't stuck around to keep me full. Come to think of it, I'd been pretty consistently hungry since the funeral, though I'd been ignoring it.

"Tala," I said, curious if she'd felt the same. She

and I normally ate very little, with Meda eating the lion's share.

"What?" she asked, her tone tinged with irritation.

I swallowed back a snarky retort and forced a smile to my face. "Have you been eating more?"

Her jaw paused mid-chew. "Yes, actually."

"It just occurred to me, when I realized how delicious those sandwiches look. I've been hungry far more often since we lost our elements."

Tala looked amazed as she stared at her ham sandwich. "You're right. You know, I always suspected my water sustained me. I never eat much. Neither do you. And Meda's always eating, but I thought maybe her fire ate at her energy where ours supplemented ours."

Meda nodded. "I don't think I've been as hungry, now you mention it."

"Well, now we know." I grabbed a sandwich and dug in as Noah and Gino walked in the door. "Where've you two been?" I asked after I swallowed.

Noah kissed my cheek. "Hey," he murmured. "Trying to get to know each other."

I realized they were both sweaty. "Oh?" I raised my eyebrow and gave them both a hard look. "In what way?"

"Tennis, actually," Gino said, then leaned over to mimic Noah's kiss. "I'm a skilled tennis player."

"And I'm a lycan." Noah shrugged. "So, faster than the witch."

Gino nodded. "Yeah, but who won?"

Noah's narrowed eyes was the only answer I needed. Gino beat Noah.

Giggling, I looked between them. "Friendly match?"

Noah's expression softened. "Yeah. Friendly."

Good.

Meda pushed her plate away, surprisingly leaving half a sandwich on it. "Let's go," she said.

"Where do we want to do this?" I asked. "Can we do it here?"

Tala scoffed. "We have a gorgeous tropical island. Why do anything inside?"

Her attitude stunk, but she wasn't wrong. "Let me leave a note for Harper," I said, grabbing some of the hotel stationery. "Only Poppy would put hotel stationery in a magical hotel," I said.

Noah chuckled behind me. "Maybe the mermaid-dude did it."

I held up the pad of paper to show him the letterhead. "Poppy's Paradise Resort."

Grabbing the paper and pulling it closer to his

face, Noah's expression lit up in delight. "Your grand-father is the best," he crowed, then turned to the rest of our group.

I needed a name for us when we were gathered together. My sisters' mates didn't quite fit the mold of family to me yet, but 'our group' seemed so impersonal.

"He's got a byline," Noah said through laughter. "For the discerning demon. London-Paris-Remote Island."

His announcement was met with a lot of laughter and head shakes. I studied the words when he handed the notepad back. "He *is* the best," I murmured as I wrote a note for Harp, Phenex, and my parents.

Headed to the beach to train. Join us if you'd like. -A

"There." I left the note on top of the sandwiches in the middle of the table. "Let's go."

We traipsed down to the water. As soon as we hit the sand, Meda took off her shoes, and it looked so appealing I did as well. After a few minutes, so did Tala, and by the time we got to the small cove we'd used before, our entire party was shoeless.

"I sure would like to swim," Meda said. "But I don't have a suit." She cut her eyes at me. "No way

I'm doing it in my bra. Everyone already saw you do it, so it's like they've seen me anyway."

Rolling my eyes, I turned away and stretched, choosing to ignore her.

"I can conjure you a bathing suit," Gino told me. "Pretty easily."

"Yeah, I can, too," I heard Sterling say, followed by a "yup," from Fenton.

I beamed at Gino. "That's awesome."

"First, I think we should try to connect to Hell, and see what we can do with that power out here with nobody around." Meda didn't have her fire, but she was still alpha, and still had to be the boss.

Gritting my teeth, I turned back to her. "Okay. Why don't you connect this time?" *Since you two thought I did such a bad job before.*

She nodded, but her expression spoke volumes. She knew exactly why I didn't want to be the one to do it.

Closing her eyes, she sucked in a deep breath and exhaled, repeating the slow breathing for several minutes while we stood around in the heat watching her. Finally, she grunted and exhaled hard. "Why is it so hard?"

"Try doing it in the middle of a battle," I said

waspishly. I knew it was the curse making me unable to move past their harsh words.

"Amitola," Tala said in a hard voice. "Can you not let it go?"

"I'm trying." Giving her a pointed glare, I opened myself up and tried to access the part of me that connected me as one of the heirs of the Kingdom of Hell. "In theory, as direct heir, Meda should have the easiest time of this."

"Why can't Dad do it?" Tala asked, breaking my concentration.

"He's a vampire," I said. "He doesn't have the same magic we do."

"He's the heir," she argued. "If something happened to Poppy, he'd take the throne, right?"

"Not necessarily." We all stared at Fenton in surprise. "I've been studying your family," he said. "I'm a scholar, can't help myself."

"Well, what did you find?"

"Your grandmother would take on the throne. She has a considerable amount of magic in her, but only while in the Hell realm."

"I bet Dad would, too," I said. "He's probably never tried."

"Here he comes, we can ask him," Noah pointed out.

Turned out, our Fenton's information was accurate.

"I've got some crazy powers while in the Hell realm, but I never spend enough time there to figure them out." Dad shrugged. "But, for now, we need you girls on your A-game."

"If we could connect to Hell, we could use the power to run drills," I said. "But so far, it's not happening."

Tala grunted. "I'm trying."

I tried as well, and this time, I found it. "Ah," I said in satisfaction. My sisters needed to be able to connect as fast as I did, and we all three needed to get much, much faster. But there was a deep gratification in knowing they'd criticized me and I achieved our goal faster than they did.

The massive power filled me, helping chase away some of the emptiness the absence of my air left behind.

"I've got it." I looked at my sisters in triumph. "Connect with me." It was easier to have them grab hold than pull them in. When they connected, the power flowed between us, energizing and revitalizing all three of us.

"I can sense it," Dad said. "It's alluring."

"I bet if we had time, we could figure out how to

pull you in." Meda looked at her hands with a frown. "This would be so amazing if I had my fire."

She was so right. My air would've loved the intensity of our newfound Hell power. "Okay," I barked. "Let's figure out how to use it."

The curse didn't budge in the face of the power that probably created it. "It seems likely Trinity used this power to put the curse on us, to begin with," I said thoughtfully. "Perhaps it needs a different power to counteract it."

Meda nodded. "We don't know any angels."

Dad burst out laughing, followed by our entire group. "And even if we did," he said. "They'd be unlikely to help the offspring of Lucifer."

"Holy shit, Dad, they're real?" My jaw dropped and I gaped at him in amazement. I'd read novels about angels, Nephilim, and the like for years. It was a particularly favorite trope of mine.

"Well, what did you think?" Mom answered for him. "Hell exists but Heaven doesn't?"

My whole world tilted on its axis. I'd never considered that it could be.

"Of course, the stories about what happened vary and nobody can get any of them to verify the truth," Pop continued. "We've tried."

"My father is tight-lipped about the whole thing,"

Dad said, obviously frustrated. "Mom doesn't even know anything."

"Well, can we debate the history of the cosmos another day?" Tala asked. She was being a bitch again, but she was right. "We need to focus."

The power flowing through me itched to be released. "Yeah. Gino, Fenton, Sterling, can you throw energy balls at us?"

"Sure," Sterling said brightly. "I love this part."

Gino looked at him in amazement. "You love trying to hurt your mate?"

"No," he said with a laugh. "But you've not seen firsthand how powerful they are."

"It's fun to keep them on their toes," Fenton finished for his cousin. Without warning, he shot a ball of what looked like fire straight at me.

"Hey," I shouted as I ducked it. "I wasn't ready."

"That's the point," he said as he threw two more at my sisters. They ducked as well. "Figure out how to counteract them, not hide from them."

It took far more energy balls than I'd ever admit before we figured out how to shoot out a tendril of power, meeting the ball in the air and evaporating it. Or maybe absorbing it. I wasn't sure, but every time we hit one, I felt a zing of triumph, or possibly power.

Eventually, we started throwing out balls of our

own. Meda figured that one out, but Tala and I quickly mimicked her.

Our orbs of energy hit the guys' in mid-air, causing explosions. The first one made me flinch, but soon I was flinging power at them as hard as I could, the explosions bigger and brighter.

"We need to do this at night for the kids," I exclaimed as a ball of mine hit one of Gino's and neon pink sparks went everywhere.

"See if you three can make one of these balls together," Fenton said. "We'll try too."

Giggling, Meda, Tala and I hovered together, letting a ball of Hell power grow between us. The guys did the same, without the giggles. I looked around to see if I could tell how big their ball was when I realized we'd attracted a bit of a crowd. The sun beat down on our ensemble, Collective families spread out on the beach, watching our training session devolve into a fireworks show.

"Ready?" Meda called when our ball was too big to contain behind our bodies anymore. "Throw toward the water just in case the blast is as big as I think it'll be."

"Ready," Fenton called.

"On three," Tala said, then counted down. As she said three, we looked at the guys. They threw their ball of bright blue energy toward the air above the water, and we did the same. It wasn't difficult to move in unison, the power tied our thoughts together, and our bodies followed suit.

The orbs crashed into each other with a loud boom, and the ground shook under our feet. The small crowd cheered as a rainbow of sparks blasted us all. I felt a few stings of power tap at my skin, but we'd managed to throw it far enough out to keep the crowd from any harm.

"Again," a small girl yelled.

We turned to see Harper and Phenex walking toward us.

"Impressive," Phenex said. "But can you use that in battle?"

"Should you be out of bed?" I asked.

"I am much improved," he said. "Sleeping with my mates helped tremendously. Your energy helped my healing process while we rested."

Phenex's arrival sobered us, and we dispersed the crowd. We weren't there to create fireworks. We could do that for the rest of our lives. For now, we had to train for combat.

As soon as training was over, I made a beeline for my hotel room. After a scalding hot shower, I dressed in my favorite nightie and had just settled down with a book when a knock sounded at the door. Harper and Noah were off doing sentry drills, so I knew it wasn't them. Then again they wouldn't knock.

Setting my book on the bed, I got up and answered the door. My heart danced at the sight of Gino. His dark brown hair was, as usual, perfect, and his chocolate gaze lit up with desire. Without speaking, he stepped inside my room and closed the door behind him. "I've been waiting for a time to get you alone."

The fire in his gaze promised passion, and I was

so on board with it. It amazed me how we'd been able to fight our desires as long as we did. Because I'd been tempted on numerous occasions to drag him off somewhere for some mind-blowing sex.

I reached for his white button-down shirt, and he grabbed my wrist while walking me back to the bed. Excitement shot through me. I would've never imagined I loved being dominated, but as much as I let my mates do it, apparently I did. The urge to be sassy and bratty rose up, and I wondered what Gino would do if I disobeyed his silent command to submit.

Even though he was a witch and not as fast or as strong as me, he still had a dominance and power inside him. I wanted to explore that side of him.

Letting my fangs lower, I smiled so they showed. His lips twitched as he noticed them, then his gaze darkened. "You going to bite me?"

"Oh, yes. Both my vampire and my lycan want to claim you. And they will." I pushed my arms into him, and he stumbled back a step but didn't let go of my wrists.

He chuckled and claimed my mouth in an unforgiving, raw kiss that sent a zap of power through me. Was that me or him? I didn't care because it felt too damn good.

Biting my lip, he pushed, and we fell on the bed in a tangle. Holding my hands above my head in one of his, he ran his other one down my side until he cupped me over my panties. A groan escaped me as I rocked my hips into his touch, wanting more.

He broke the kiss and trailed his lips to my ear. "As much as I want to tease every part of you, I need to be inside you now."

"Yes!" I tried to move my hands but he tightened his grip. I could break his hold if I wanted to. But a wickedly naughty part of me wanted to see where he was going to take this.

He brushed my panties to the side and thrust two fingers inside me, making me cry out in pleasure. My orgasm slammed into me, the intensity of the first time with my new mate taking me high. I desperately wanted to touch him, but he didn't release my hands.

Yanking down my panties, he pushed them down my legs until I was able to kick out of them. Then he tried to remove his pants with one hand. I smirked. "If you release my hands I could help."

"Oh no. You touch me, and I'll be done for." Gino's lips lifted into a sensual smile, and I almost came again.

Giving up on removing his pants, he settled for

pulling himself out of his pants and scooting them down enough to grip his hard and huge cock as he guided it to my entrance. With a quick thrust, he entered me. Pleasure and desire crashed together and another release exploded inside me as he stretched me to the point of pain. If he'd been a fraction of an inch bigger, or if I hadn't been soaking wet, it would've been really painful.

He held on to my wrist with both his hands as he moved in and out, each forward thrust taking him deeper. My climax built higher, rolling through me like shockwaves. I wrapped my legs around his waist and rocked my hips with his once he made it fully inside, my walls stretching to accommodate him.

His scent filled my senses, clouding all ability to think. I was running on primal instinct and the need to claim him. Lifting my head, I struck, sinking my fangs into the curve of his neck, even with my hands trapped above me. His rich, magical blood coated my tongue and slid down my throat. I moaned as I sucked, taking what I needed.

Mine. He was mine.

The threads of a bond formed and weaved together faster than it had with Harper and Noah. Gino picked up his tempo, pounding into me while keeping his neck still under my teeth. My skin heated and tingled while our minds merged as the mating bond between us took root. When it snapped in place, we both cried out as our release washed over us.

Only then did he release my hands. I slid my arms around his neck and kissed him. When I broke it he stared down at me. Smiling, I asked, "What?"

"You are so beautiful."

"So are you."

He frowned. "Handsome, maybe."

I stroked his cheek with my index finger. "Men can be beautiful."

"I guess." He winked at me and pulled out. Then he rolled to his side, taking me with him.

After he kicked his pants off, I settled over Gino's chest with our legs tangled together. Listening to the *thump, thump* of his heart while feeling him inside my head. Our bond was strong, and I knew Harper and Noah had felt it snap in place. Harper wasn't happy about it, but she couldn't do anything about it, even if I'd wanted her to.

Gino stroked my shoulder with his fingers. "Now I know what Sterling was talking about when he said you and your sisters were powerful. I couldn't imagine carrying around that much power."

"I guess we're used to it. And it seems to be still growing."

Rumbling voices out in the common area made me frown. Then Meda entered my thoughts. *Tala had a vision. We need to go. Now.*

What? I jumped up and quickly dressed. "Something is wrong."

Gino was dressed and at the door before I was. Not impressive considering he'd never even taken off his shirt. We exited the room, and I crossed the common area to my sisters. "What is it?"

Meda had tears in her eyes. "Kins. Trinity has her."

Immediately, I start to form a portal, picking at threads to take us to her parents' home. Mom held up her hand. "Stop. We don't know what we're walking into."

The *niswi* each stared at her and asked, "We?"

Mom ignored them. "You can't go charging in unprepared."

"Mom, this is Kins and her family!" Meda began to pace.

With a sigh, Mom said, "I know, honey, but we don't even know where she is. They went to their secret place and only their secret keeper knows."

Meda stopped. "I know a few that might know. People close to her family."

Her lycan mate, Peter said, "Write the names down and I'll see if they are on the island and ask around."

Noah entered the suite and crossed the room with Harper and Randell behind him. "I'll help." He'd heard, apparently.

Meda nodded and grabbed the stationary pad and pen, then went to the table to make the list of names for Peter and Noah.

Harper stopped next to me and brushed her fingers against my hand. Wrapping my pinky with hers, I focused on the group. "We need a plan while the guys are hunting down the secret keeper."

Mom nodded. "Tala, tell us everything in your vision."

Tala leaned into Kevin, and he wrapped his arms around her. "Trinity has them tied up. She used the curse she placed on us to tap into my visions somehow to send us a message. She said for us to come to her or Kins and her family will die."

Mom cursed. "She's a crazy bitch. We know this a trap and I wouldn't put past her to have already..."

"Jilly," Papa warned. Then he turned to us. "We go in knowing it's a trap, but that doesn't help us with the battle. Trinity is harnessing Hell power. What else do we know?"

"She wants revenge on all of us it seems." Tala crossed her arms and bit her lips.

I glanced up and met Phenex's stare as he walked in. "Phenex, can you call the hounds to help?"

"I will."

"Phenex, we'll need you to hang back to control the portals. We're not as fast at creating them as you." Meda rejoined us in the center of the common area. Peter and Noah left to find out where Kins's family's secret hideaway was.

Phenex nodded.

Mom met each of our stares. "Go in working as a team. Try like hell to fight the negative effects of the curse. Trinity will use it against you."

We nodded. And I sent a silent prayer to Poppy that Kins and her family were okay.

CHAPTER FIFTEEN

*P*henex disappeared to gather his hounds. I didn't like to see him leave when the last time he'd left the realm it had been a trap, but he'd promised to pop directly into Hell and back.

Meda, Tala, and I took turns pacing the living room. After a half-hour, the three of us had to promise not to speak until we got news, because every time we did, we ended up yelling at each other.

Our *niswi* took mom into their bedroom to escape our venom. Several times one of us tried to leave the room and sit alone to wait, but always came back. Our nerves were too much on edge.

Finally, Phenex returned, walking through the

hall. "They're in the hall," he said. "I didn't want to leave a portal to Hell open any longer than I had to."

Nodding, I sat on the edge of the couch and watched the door for the return of Peter and Noah.

Voices outside the door alerted us to their presence a moment before they walked in. "Here you go," Noah said. "Kinsley's grandmother."

He held his arm out, and an older woman with black hair streaked silver, walked in. "What's going on?" she asked, bowing at my mom as she stepped out of the bedroom. Her hair was rumpled like she'd grabbed a nap.

She'd been super-sleepy through the pregnancies of all our siblings. "Hello," she said kindly to the older woman. "I'm Jillian."

"Constance," she replied, looking around. "Why am I here?" Her wide eyes held a considerable amount of fear. "All they'd say is you needed to speak to me. Is this about my family?"

Tala stepped forward, and I felt her magic pulse in the bond. She was probably feeling Constance's fear. Her empathy was difficult for her to block sometimes. "Constance, we fear Kinsley is in danger."

Constance shook her head. "Can't be. They went to their hidden home."

"That's sort of the point. We think that their

home has been discovered." I gave Constance a sympathetic look before continuing. "I know it's a lot to ask, but we need to check on them."

"I can't," she said.

"What if you tell me?" I asked. "We can step into the other room, and I can open a portal that is big enough for us to peek through, just like a peephole on a door. If everything looks normal, I'll swear to keep the secret and we'll move on."

She considered my offer and nodded. "Okay, yeah. We can just check first."

We walked into my bedroom, and after she whispered the location in my ear, I found the place where I could pluck at the tapestry. In no time, I had a tiny hole open and held the strands away from each other with my mind. Peering through the hole, I saw blood all over the walls.

Releasing the threads with a snap, I turned to Constance. "Are you here alone?"

"No, my husband, son, and his family are here."

"Do they know you're here?"

She nodded, her face moving from fear to sheer terror. "What did you see? Let me see."

"I've already closed the portal." I opened the door to the others. "Constance, go to your family. Wait downstairs. We might be gone a while. It didn't look good. We have to go get your daughter and grand-daughter."

Meda sucked in a deep breath, squaring her shoulders.

"I'll walk her down," Mom said. "I'm not going with you." Tears filled her eyes as she spoke. She put her hands on my shoulders and kissed my forehead. "Be strong."

Moving to Tala, she said, "Be fast." Then, to Meda, "Be sure."

I felt my sisters' sadness as they watched Mom say goodbye to the *niswi*, then walk out the door with Constance, her head held high. It took a great deal of strength for her to not watch us go through and maybe even watch from the portal.

But she was a leader of all the Collective, not just her family. She had to be there for Kinsley's family as well.

"Are we ready?" I asked as I looked around at my *niswi*, mates, and sentries. The hounds stood in the hall peering in, none of them familiar to me.

Nobody said anything in argument, so I prepared to open the portal. "Stand back," I said.

"Hang on," Meda said. "Let's get the power flowing before we go in."

I nodded and started trying to connect to the hell

power we'd *have* to have to make any headway against Trinity.

As usual, I connected first. They were going to have to start practicing. What if something happened and they needed it while I wasn't around? I grabbed them and pushed the power into them without preamble. When we were filled as full as we could be, I slashed open the portal, Meda conjuring a sword for her and Tala. I followed, forming energy balls and shooting them off before I'd even gone through the portal.

The living room was covered in blood, and once I got a proper look at it, I realized three bodies laid on the floor. "Check them," I yelled as I flung energy balls at the demons pouring from the back of the house. I hadn't imagined that many demons could fit inside a house that looked like it was maybe a three-bedroom, if that. But they kept coming.

Phenex stooped and put his hands on the bodies of Kinsley and her parents. I knew what he was going to say before he opened his mouth. "They're dead," he said sadly.

My heart clenched in my chest and Meda whispered, "No."

I shoved my grief away. Meda and Tala kept the demons away from us, and away from the bodies of our friends, but I didn't know how long they could keep the demons on that side of the room. The *niswi* fought well, helping Meda and Tala keep the demons at bay, but there were too many of them. "Get them out of here. Find an empty room in the hotel for them and tell mom. Then come right back. Don't say anything in front of Kinsley's grandmother."

Phenex nodded, and made a portal beside the bodies. I looked away as he picked up Kinsley and stepped through. Focusing on throwing fireballs, I intentionally didn't watch the removal of the bodies.

When Phenex returned, Dad spoke up. "Get in the back and be prepared to open a portal to get us out of here if necessary." Phenex nodded and moved toward the back of the room.

Maniacal laughter echoed around us. "Welcome," Trinity's voice said. "I've been expecting you."

"Come out and face us, you bitch," Tala growled. "Stop hiding behind your demons."

"Where is your father?" I heard my Paw ask Dad. "Why is he allowing all these demons to be under her control?"

"I don't know. I haven't been able to reach him since he set us up on the island."

I kept throwing the energy balls while my sisters

swung their swords. Our sentries tried to edge around us and protect us, but they just couldn't get past us. We were better than they were. If a demon got around us, they dispatched it with ease.

As I thought about how well we were doing, I realized I'd been backing up. The sheer volume of demons was slowly backing us toward the portal. I had to let it go and trust Phenex to be prepared to get us out now that he knew where we were. Inch by inch, we were pressed toward the door. The hounds in the back opened it. I looked when I felt the atmosphere in the room change. The air from the breeze outside caressed my cheek as if telling me it missed me. With a sob, I soaked up more power, throwing more and more energy balls.

When they hit their mark, which wasn't as often as they should have, they didn't seem to have the same effect as the last time. These demons were warded or shielded somehow. The sword, or physical contact, worked fine.

Magic, not so much.

By the time we retreated to the front porch, my energy waned. I started pulling from my mates, minuscule amounts to help me continue funneling the power. I was afraid I'd have to switch to hand-to-hand combat to keep myself in the game.

"Meda," I called. "Conjure me two swords, please."

She knew exactly what I wanted. I liked having two smaller swords in-hand, to slice and dice.

I kept hold of the hell power but didn't try to focus it. I dug into the demons with a gusto. Some of them disintegrated, some fell with a squelch. Some had horns, others had spikes. They were as varied as the animals in the forest or the faces of the humans. Each one unique.

Each one had to die.

Soon I realized it wasn't going well. Just as I thought about calling a retreat, or at least encouraging Meda or the *niswi* to call one, a roar from the forest behind us had me whirling around.

We kept fighting, but our attention kept straying to the forest, especially when the ground shook under our feet.

"What the hell is that?" Tala yelled as she chopped the head off of a demon with purple spikes.

We didn't have to wait long to find out. It stomped out of the forest, with the head of a lion. "Holy Hell," I whispered, my swords dropping to my side as I took in its massive horns.

Big mistake. As soon as my arms dropped, something plowed into my side. I hit the ground hard with a grunt.

Someone yanked the demon off of me, giving me time to get to my feet, but I gasped in pain. It felt like my ribs were cracked.

Tears rolled down my cheeks as I forced myself to stand. My magic would heal them in a few hours, but I had to fight in the meantime.

I cried out as I slashed a demon just in time to keep it from stabbing Harper in the back with its massive claws.

The hounds had circled, but with the appearance of the horned creature, they redirected their attention to it.

"You three focus on the Nian," Dad yelled. Apparently, the creature had a name. A Nian. "We'll hold the demons back."

Meda, Tala, and I retreated behind the hounds, and they turned to help keep the demons off us. I tried to ignore the bodies on the ground. If I stopped to see who they were, I might not be able to continue.

Pulling on the power inside me, I tried sending a stream of blistering magic at the creature, funneling the power straight from Hell and into the face of the behemoth.

It roared in pain and charged. "Look out," I yelled

as we jumped out of its way. It went berserk, stampeding and trampling anyone or anything in its path.

"We have to retreat," I yelled. "Phenex, get us out of here!"

A portal opened up in front of me. I had no idea where my mate was, but he could at least hear me.

I flailed my swords, keeping demons at bay. "Come on," I yelled. "*niswi*, Harper, Noah! Gino!"

Meda and Tala called the same. "Phenex," Meda screamed. "Tell the hounds to go."

Without warning, several portals opened, and the hounds fled through them. "Don't let the demons through the portals!" I yelled as I saw a demon jump thought behind a hound. "Kill them if they come through."

My sisters and I helped the sentries keep the demons at bay—barely—so the bodies of the wounded could be dragged through.

Finally, there was one portal behind us. When the last body went through, we jumped through and the portal slammed shut, cutting a blue demon with nasty black horns in half.

"Oh, gross." I whirled around to see Randell punch a demon in the face in the middle of our common area, then Tala ran it through with her sword. Turning in quick circles, I looked for my mates and saw Meda and Tala running to their own. One of the *niswi's* sentries laid on the floor, almost certainly dead. Dad had a huge gash on his forehead that poured blood. Mom was fussing over him, splitting her attention between pressing a cloth to the cut and looking him over for more.

"Ami," Gino said behind me. I clutched my ribs. Now that the adrenaline was crashing, the ribs hurt a lot worse. I'd been hit more times than I realized. Blood oozed from a cut on my arm.

Gino sat against the wall, holding his leg. He'd been stabbed. The knife was still in it. "Can anyone do anything about this?" I asked.

Phenex stumbled forward. "I'm sorry," he said. "I wanted to help, but I had to be available to get everyone out."

"It's okay, can you just heal it?"

"I don't have much healing power," he said. "But without Meda's fire, I might be the only one with any."

He pulled the knife out and focused, and the blood slowly stopped pouring out.

"Over here," Meda called. "I think Dorian's leg is broken."

Phenex moved away, and I stood to find Harper and Noah sitting on the couch beside each other. "Are you injured?" I asked, stumbling toward them.

"Nothing life-threatening," Noah said. Harper shook her head, but she looked like crap.

"That was a disaster," I said. "We were like children."

My *niswi* nodded. "Where is all the power you three are supposed to have?" Paw asked. "What happened?"

"It's the curse," I said. "And they were fortified somehow. The magic didn't work."

"Everyone rest. Recuperate." Mom looked around the room. "Whoever is the least injured, throw those demons back to Hell."

Phenex stood. "On it." He made a portal flat on the floor, then dragged the bodies to it, letting them fall through.

Sterling stood, limping, and focused on the blood left by the demons. It disappeared.

"We'll touch base tomorrow," Mom said. "Rest now." She walked out with her arm around Paw. "I'm going to tell Constance what happened."

My heart splintered, and I felt guilty for not offering to go with her, but the thought of seeing Kinsley's grandmother's face as Mom broke the news was more than I could face just then.

CHAPTER SIXTEEN

I laid tangled with my sisters and Phenex for what seemed liked hours. We'd all suffered some pretty severe injuries. But being with our hound, our center, wasn't helping like it had with him. I wasn't sure why.

"Nothing is happening," Meda groaned out.

"Maybe we need all our mates," Tala said. Her tone was low, and I felt her fatigue and pain. I felt the same.

I was pretty sure I had bruises in places that no one was ever supposed to get bruises. "I feel like I'm missing them, like a limb lost." My eyes welled with tears, my heart aching to be near them.

Meda grunted. "It's worth a shot."

At least I'd feel better cuddled up with my three mates, plus Phenex.

Meda twisted to reach for her phone on the nightstand, groaning in the process. She sent a group text, including all thirteen of us. "We're going to need a group message eventually. Let's move to the common area."

We nodded but no one moved for several moments. A knock on Phenex's door put us in motion. Meda was the first to the door and opened it. It was Randell, but I could see Harper and Noah behind him. Meda pointed to the common area. "We have a theory that if all thirteen of us sleep together we'll heal faster."

She pushed past Randell, not giving him time to respond. It also said she's wasn't in the mood to argue. I fought back the need to lash out at her for being rude. Then, I remembered that it was the curse that made us snippy and angry.

When I walked into the common area, the guys had begun pulling the mattresses from our rooms and placing them on the floor. The furniture had been moved to the far wall to give us plenty of room. They'd worked fast. I appreciated it. They were just as sore as we were.

I sensed Gino moments before he entered the

suite. We locked gazes, and I frowned as his pain flowed through our bond. He limped over to me and I reached out, taking his hand in mine. Harper closed the distance to me. I gave her a sharp look as her tension seeped through the bond. She wasn't jealous of Gino, but she was still wary of him.

Sighing, Harper kissed my cheek. "I'm trying."

"Try harder," I snapped and then sat down on the mattress next to Noah. I wasn't going to put up with a divide between my mates. It would do nothing but put extra stress on me. That was the last thing I needed to deal with.

When I saw the hurt look on her face, I felt like an ass. "I'm sorry. It's this curse. I don't mean it." She nodded but still looked hurt.

Gino settled down beside me, curling into my back. Harper stared down at us for several moments before wedging herself between me and Noah, leaving enough room for Noah to curl around her and still rest his head beside mine. He touched his forehead to mine.

I watched Phenex move around the large makeshift bed. He gave me a small smile before slipping in next to Noah. Meda and her mates curled up in the center. Tala and her mates took up the other end. I reached over Harper and Noah, making them wedge closer together, and put my hand on Phenex's back. As I scooted away from Gino, he scooted with me, staying pressed into my back.

Then Phenex said, "As weird as it may seem, it would be best if we touched our neighbor in some way. The point of this is to for us to connect and help each other heal."

Randell growled. "Kevin, that's my ass."

"Sorry, mate." Kevin chuckled, then said wiggled. "Oh, that's better."

I started giggling, which had an infectious effect. Harper giggled, then my sisters.

It took us several minutes before we settled down and pushed away the laughter. Slowly, I listened to my family fall asleep, grunts and groans replaced with steady breathing. I was the last one to drift off to sleep.

I woke the next morning—well late-morning—feeling great. I still had some soreness, but my bruises were gone and my cuts were already scabbed over. Nothing like the power of your mates. Everyone else was still asleep, except for a couple of empty spots. Gino wasn't there, or Randell.

Curling up in a chair next to the window, I sipped my coffee and watched the waves crash onto the shore as I thought about Kinsley. We'd failed her.

Gino's scent curled around me like a warm hug. Then he kissed my cheek. "Morning."

"Morning."

He picked me up, almost making me spill my coffee. Then he sat in the chair with me in his lap. "I figured we could spend the day together."

The thought of spending time with him made me happy. "What did you have in mind?"

He shrugged. "Lunch. Then go for a walk, see what mischief we can get into."

I lifted both my brows. "Oh, really?" It sounded perfect. A great distraction from my morose thoughts.

I was more intrigued with getting into trouble than I normally would be. Probably because of the curse. Then again, I could've been picking up on his bad boy side through our link.

Standing, I moved to the sink and set my cup in it. Gino waited for me by the door while I changed clothes in my mattress-less room.

In the elevator on the way down, he linked our hands together and pulled me into him. I sighed, feeling his emotions through our bond. There was a mix of desire, lust, and affection. He was also intrigued with me like he wanted to know everything about me. But that was a two-way street. Bond or no bond.

We exited the elevator hand in hand and he directed us to the kitchen. I watched as he pulled fresh herbs and tomatoes out of the fridge. He divided the tomatoes between us and handed me a knife. "Dice those, please."

I start dicing as he got a large pot and set it between us. I lifted my gaze to study his profile. "I thought we were going to stir up trouble."

He chuckled. "We will." He winked and added, "We do need to eat."

Yes, we did, and I was starving. "What are we making?"

"Sauce for chicken parmesan." He went to the large walk-in pantry and grabbed some onions.

"Oh! With homemade sauce."

He rolled his eyes. "It's the only sauce I'll eat."

Of course. He was Italian, after all. My sexy Italian.

When we finished chopping everything and adding it to the pot, he put it on the stove to simmer. "We probably shouldn't go far."

I nodded, agreeing with him. We walked out to a beautiful courtyard and sat at a table that overlooked the ocean. The smell of the salt in the air made me miss my element. I would have loved to know what secrets were mixed in the sea breeze.

Gino reached over the table and touched my hand. I turned my palm over and linked our hands together. He studied me for a few moments. "Are you okay?"

"Yeah. Just miss my air element. It's so much of who I am, I don't like that it's not there." I stuck my lip out and glanced down to our hands. "You don't even know me with it." I sucked in a deep breath. "And I'm worried about Kinsley's grandmother. Mom went to break the news to her last night. It can't have gone well."

He moved his chair so that it butted against mine. "I'm sorry about your friend. And I wish I knew how to break the curse, but that is out of my area of expertise."

I studied his features for several long moments. "Is your family really some kind of mob?" Changing the subject was the best idea, or I'd start to bawl.

His eyes lifted to meet mine and a wicked smile formed. "As in underground crime lords dealing in illegal actives? No."

He paused for a few seconds, then added, "some of the potions and spells we deal in may cross the gray area of witch law, but they are sold and used with only good intentions."

A laugh burst from me. He was *so* a witch version of a mobster. "What is your role in your non-mob circle?"

Playfulness flashed across his face and he poked my side. I jerked, expecting to feel pain from our battle yesterday. There was none. He watched me, and I sensed his concern through our bond. When he didn't comment on my reaction, I figured he'd also sensed my emotions.

He draped an arm on the back of my chair. "I'm the heir of our circle and future mob boss." He leaned in close and pressed his lips to my cheek.

I giggled, knowing he added the latter to tease me about my suspicions. "So you will take your mom's place in ordering hits on people?"

He threaded his hand in my hair and pulled, bring my head back so he could kiss my throat. "We don't put hits of people. We don't outsource the killing of rogues."

"Yeah, I can see your mother being an assassin."

He chuckled and bit down on my neck, drawing a half-groan, half-squeak from me. "Stop," I hissed, looking around.

He chuckled and sat up straight, but didn't take his arm off of me. I didn't mind.

"Seriously though, outsiders do label us as a mob family. It's how we operate because we have some extremely powerful witches in our circle and that power needs to be managed differently. It requires secrecy, strict rules, and strict consequences."

I could see that. "I'm not judging. My grandfather is Satan. I'm pretty sure he invented the art of torture."

He let go of me and stood. I missed his touch and almost reached out to him. Curiously, I found comfort in his dominant, commanding nature. Leaning down, he pressed his lips to mine. "I'm going to check on the sauce."

Smiling I nodded. "I'll be here."

He disappeared into the kitchen and that was when I noticed my Dad lurking in the shadows, near the corner of the building. Frowning, I wondered how long he'd been there and why the hell I hadn't noticed him. "Stalking us, Dad?"

He advanced to the table and sat in Gino's chair. We sat in silence for several moments, staring at each other. Through our bond, I sensed his confliction, but I didn't say anything. If he was going to lecture me on mating Gino, then he was better off leaving. I didn't want to hear it, and I wasn't going to push Gino away. He was my mate.

"I hadn't realized that you'd bonded with the witch yet. Too much going on." Dad stared out over the ocean. I knew he was busy watching the Collective and possible threats to our people. He was, however, the High King. "I also have misjudged him without getting to know him."

I turned in my seat and stared at Dad. "How long were you lurking?"

Dad smirked. "I wasn't lurking." He tapped my nose. "And you need to be more alert to your surroundings. Gino knew I was here." I heard the unspoken rest of his sentence. *And he's just a witch.*

Not that there was anything less about being a witch, but they didn't have the innate senses of the vampires and Lycans. "Hmm." I straightened in my chair and brought my knees to my chest. I was like that with Harper and Noah too. They were my sentries and always on alert for threats. I felt safe with them as I did with Gino. "What did you learn by stalking us?"

Dad chuckled and pulled me in a hug. The arm of my chair bit into my side, but I didn't say anything. We didn't get many moments to just be father and daughter. Not with all the evil crap we'd been dealing with. "I learned that Gino is perfect for you. I wasn't aware until Sterling told me about how much power the Dragos manage within their circle. It makes more sense now."

I lifted my head. "Thanks, Dad." He had accepted Gino. Maybe not fully, but he was starting to, and that was good enough for me. For now. "How are you feeling? How are Paw and Papa?"

"We're healing at our own speed. We don't want to pull too much power from your mother. This pregnancy and the stress are draining her." He sighed then kissed my forehead. Then he stood and glanced to Gino, who stood at the entrance of the kitchen and nodded. "Try to rest today."

"I will." I didn't mention that I felt way better than normal. I wasn't sure I understood why. Maybe my injuries weren't as severe as I first thought. "You do the same."

Gino and I spent another half an hour or so sitting in the courtyard talking about our siblings. He had three younger brothers. And Gino had gone to law school to study human business law.

When the chicken parmesan was ready, we moved to the kitchen, and I ate until I was stuffed. "That was amazing."

Gino grinned. "Thank you. It'll be even better

tomorrow. The sauce needs time to set." He stared at me then asked how my injuries were. "I sense no pain from you, which is good. Is that normal healing speed for you?"

I shrugged. "I did seem to heal faster than usual. Then again I could have felt worse than it really was last night."

Now that he mentioned it, I didn't sense any pain from him, either. And he wasn't walking with a limp. Dad was right, I needed to focus more on my surroundings. "How about you?"

"Surprisingly, I'm pretty much healed. I've never healed so fast. Ever. It was like all thirteen of us sleeping together had some kind of magical..." He stopped talking, and his jaw dropped. His eyes grew round like he was having a light bulb moment. "Oh. Ami, we're so stupid." Gino clenched his fists. "Stupid!"

"What?" I asked bewildered. The date had gone well. What had happened that I didn't notice? What did I miss?

He jumped up and grabbed my hand. "It's all thirteen. *You need all thirteen.*"

"What do you mean?" Gino was nuts. "We've all been connected. It didn't help."

"No, we haven't." He shook his head. "Every time we've tried to connect the three of you with all your mates, at least one person wasn't there for one reason or another."

He was right. We came close when during the disaster of a rescue attempt for Kinsley, but Phenex had held back to make portals. When we trained, we hadn't had everyone present, so even if we'd tried, it wouldn't have worked.

"Do you think this could break the curse?" My blood pumped with excitement. If it worked, the black tar corrupting my mind might finally disappear. Imagining my air flowing through me again made me feel a hundred pounds lighter. I could float away at the thought of it.

"It's entirely possible," he said. He leaned across the table and took my hand. "We need to try."

"If this works, I can go back to not eating like a maniac," I said.

Gino smiled. "Isn't eating a good thing?"

I shrugged. "Yes, of course, but I don't eat much. I don't need much. Neither does Tala. It's like our elements sustain us. In contrast, Meda eats a ton. We think her fire burns up her energy and she needs more sustenance than we do."

"You ready?"

He nodded. "Let's get everyone gathered and test my theory."

We walked toward the beach, to the same spot we'd been training. On the way, I texted my sisters.

Gino had an idea. Gather all the mates. Everyone. No exceptions. Beach.

I sent a similar message to Harper and Noah, then we sat near the water and waited.

Harper and Meda turned up first. Judging by their clothes, they'd been jogging on the beach. I smiled at them, squashing the flash of irritation at seeing my mate and sister together. Normal-Ami would never be irritated at that. Harper and Meda had jogged together since we were kids, and probably always would. They were friends, just like Tala was friends with Meda's mate, Peter. And though we weren't close, Randell and I had been known to watch a movie together or read in the same room. He didn't want to spread it around, but he enjoyed a lot of the same books I did. They weren't particularly manly, and he was afraid the guys would give him a hard time.

So, when the irritation flared, I pushed it away. It was just the curse.

"What's the big idea?" Harper asked. I was proud that I didn't see one flash of jealousy from her.

She plopped down beside us. "I hope it's a good one, cause I'm starting to feel a freak out coming."

Meda snorted. "Same."

I looked at Gino. "It was your brainwave. Want to tell them or wait for everyone?"

He grinned. "Make them suffer?"

The water lapped closer as the tide came in. It was almost to our toes. "I agree." I took off my shoes and socks, then turned my head around to look at Meda, sitting behind us on the beach. "Suffer," I hissed, twisting my face into a comically crazy expression as I tossed my shoes well up the beach, away from the incoming tide.

She couldn't help but laugh at me. "You must have a great idea if you're in this good of a mood."

Randell and Tala came into view down the beach as the water touched my toes. I giggled and wiggled them in the wet sand.

"There's Phenex, walking with Fenton and Sterling," Meda said, shielding her eyes. "And there's Dorian with Kevin." She squinted. "Peter and Noah are bringing up the rear."

That was all of us. Maybe we should've invited our parents there for the big moment, but it felt almost private. This was our time. If it worked, it would be our big moment. A way we could defeat the massive threat against us. Against our people.

She'd killed too many people. Trinity had to die.

When everyone joined us, Gino stood and held his hand out to me. Of course, I didn't need help standing, but a hand up from the sand was a sweet gesture. It told me he'd been thinking about me as much as the news he was excited to deliver.

"Okay, I know I'm new here, and as the last to join the group, let me just say, you could've given a warmer welcome." He grinned broadly to show his good humor.

"He's joking, but he's right," I said. I did not smile. They'd been cool toward him at best. Hell, even I had.

Meda pursed her lips in a look of contrition. "We'll make sure to make up for it once our lives are back to normal." She reached out and squeezed his arm. "Welcome to the family. Now, will you please tell us the big news?"

Tala narrowed her eyes and blurted out a question as Gino opened his mouth to speak. "Are you pregnant?"

"What?" I exclaimed. "No, of course not! Will you hush and let him tell you what he figured out?"

She closed her mouth, but her expression didn't change.

I rolled my eyes and looked at my newest mate. His brown eyes flashed and he opened his mouth to speak again, pausing for a split-second to make sure nobody wanted to interrupt him again. "So, we were all pretty beaten up just yesterday. Trinity and her demons—and that Nian—wiped the floor with us."

Randell grunted, looking supremely irritated. Tala scowled, and Meda opened her mouth.

I held up a finger and shot her a warning look. *Let him continue.* I wouldn't interrupt him by reprimanding her out loud, but I'd gladly do it in her head.

Sorry, but we need to have a serious convo with the niswi *about that Nian.*

I rolled my eyes and nodded, but didn't respond.

Gino wasn't fooled. He waited until my gaze returned to him. "Finished?"

I nodded, shoulders sinking. My attempt to not interrupt him hadn't worked after all.

"So, we woke up this morning, after all thirteen of us slept in close quarters with each other, mostly healed." He rolled his shoulders and flexed his muscles. "Anybody still significantly hurt?"

I did the same, checking the muscles in my body to see if any pain hit me. "We're fast healers anyway," I said, just to play the devil's advocate.

"You are, yes, but some of our injuries were significant. Besides, Fenton, Sterling, and I aren't. We heal at the same rate as humans if we don't have magical intervention."

"I'm sorry," Meda said. "If I had my power I could've helped."

Peter put his arm around her while Gino smiled at her. "Thank you. But look at us. The worst of our cuts are small and scabbed over." He pointed at Fenton. "Didn't you have a broken rib?"

Fenton nodded. "Yeah, and it's just kinda bruised now." I'd had a broken rib for sure, and barely felt it now.

"And vampires heal fast, but a broken leg overnight?" He pointed at Dorian, who'd had a broken leg the day before.

"I was pretty sure my ankle was severely sprained. Maybe even a muscle or ligament injury. I was going to ask for the shaman today. But it's fine. Like it never happened." Gino rolled his ankle to show it didn't hurt. "I believe it's because all thirteen of us slept together. We likely shared power and healing in our sleep, the way Phenex healed when he was injured."

The reactions from the group ranged from instant acceptance—Phenex—to confusion—Tala—to surprised delight—Fenton. Fenton's eyes lit up. "And if all thirteen of us makes such a difference while we sleep—"

Meda gasped. "What will it do while we're holding the immense power of Hell?"

Gino grinned in triumph. "Exactly. Anybody game to try?"

"*Hell* yeah!" Tala crowed.

"Okay, come here." I held my hands out to my sisters. "It might be easier if we touch. "Phenex, in the middle."

We circled our hound, clasping hands around him. "Should we touch him?" Tala asked. "He's our catalyst, right?"

Phenex shrugged. "Do what feels natural."

I let go of Meda and Tala and stepped closer to Phenex, wrapping my arms around him. My sisters did the same.

Turning my head and resting it on Phenex's arm, I looked at my mates. "Felt right." They gave me amused looks.

"Okay," I said, taking charge. It didn't always have to be Meda. "Let's do this slowly. We don't know exactly what will happen." Sucking in a deep breath, I tried to find my connection to Hell. It was a slippery bastard. "If someone connects, say something."

I'd been the one to connect the fastest so far. Probably because I'd done it more. This time, Meda surprised us. "Got it," she called from the other side of Phenex. Tala grinned at me, her ear pressed to Phenex's chest. "Pull us in, Meda," she said. I hadn't seen such a pure, excited look on her face since before Elijah died.

The positioning of our bodies meant her boobs were squished into my arm. I wiggled my arm, remembering the phase we'd gone through in high school. "Remember when we'd hide and punch each other in the boobs?"

She snorted, but couldn't reply. Meda connected to us and power rushed into me. I closed my eyes and breathed deep. She'd already pulled Phenex in. "Okay," I said, my voice echoing in our heads as well as out in the salty beach air. "One at a time now. Let's get the witches first. "Sterling." I ignored the murky black of the curse, snaking around like a blob of flying black jello.

Opening my eyes, I watched Sterling step forward and put his hand on Meda's back. As he touched her, he popped into my consciousness, as if joining us in a room in another realm. Shoot, as much as we truly knew about this, maybe that's exactly what it was. The addition of his inherent power increased my capacity to hold power marginally. That was a good sign. I didn't think we'd connected in this way before, one at a time.

"Fenton," I called. When he touched Tala, my power increased again. "Every time someone joins us, I feel my capacity to hold power increase, as if there's a jar inside me, and the jar holds magic. Every time one of you connects, the jar grows bigger and fills with more power." Unfortunately, the curse seemed to grow as well, filling the background of our minds.

"That's a perfect analogy of this," Meda said. "I noticed it, too."

"Me, three," Tala said, turning her head away from me to look at Meda.

"Gino?" I asked, and he touched my back. When he did, the jar grew considerably larger. "Ohhh," I breathed.

Tala flipped her head around on Phenex's chest. "That was a big difference."

"We've been connected like this before," Meda said. "And never noticed."

"Yeah, but not one at a time. It was more obvious this way."

"Okay, who wants to go next?" I asked, still taking the lead.

"Me," Dorian said, sounding excited.

I nodded and smiled at him, so he stepped forward.

Vampires and Lycans had magic, for sure, but it wasn't the active kind of witches. When he joined, the imaginary jar grew, but not as much as it had with each witch. The process repeated with Kevin and Harper. I smiled at her over my shoulder.

"Okay, moment of truth," I said. "Peter?"

It was getting hard to see everyone with most of the mates circling us so close. I didn't see him put his hand on Meda's back, but I felt it. He popped into my mind, and the power increase was about the same as the vampires. Randell stepped forward without being asked, then I looked at Noah. "Ready?"

He nodded.

"This is the moment of truth," I said.

"I'm so excited," Gino said. Everyone laughed. I loved seeing this silly side of him. He'd been cocky before, but this was a streak of child-like behavior that was sexy on him.

The instant Noah touched my back, the jar shattered into a million pieces. Meda, Tala, and I cried out in unison. Power flowed through us, more than we'd ever held before. The amount we'd wrangled during the battle with Calista suddenly felt like child's play.

"Shit," Gino whispered behind me. "I can't control any of it, but I can feel it." He panted behind me. "How are you controlling it?"

"I have no idea."

Phenex, who had been quiet for the whole thing, spoke up. "You can't hold this level of power. You've got to let it out."

"Meda," I said, the power inside me beginning to make my skin feel tight. "He's right."

"Take control, Meda," Tala said. Meda had more

witchy powers than Tala or I did. Tala had the visions, I had the weird time-freezing thing.

"I'm trying," she grunted. "It's not easy."

"We'll help," I said. I had no idea how, though.

Fenton groaned. "It's starting to hurt," he said, his voice strained.

I focused on the massive flow of power, like a rushing river headed through all of us. All I could do was try to will it into a tunnel. "If I had my air, maybe I could help contain the power with air pressure."

"Meda," Tala said through a gasp. "Direct it at the curse."

Redirecting the power was like trying to redirect the sun. Grab hold of the rays and push them in a certain direction.

As we had joined, the inky blackness of the curse had joined as well. It floated around us, staining the background of our psyche. I pushed at the power where it felt like Meda was. "Tala, push," I said, my voice coming out as if I were physically moving a mountain. I felt her join us, and the power began to budge. Instead of flowing up and down like a water-fall going both ways, it sprayed out onto the black magic keeping us from our elements.

The disgusting, oily curse evaporated when the magic touched it. I gasped. "More," I cried. "Fenton,

Sterling, Gino!" I clutched Gino's essence inside my head, pulling him to the edge of the tsunami of power. *Push here. Witches, push here!*

Our witches helped, more magic spraying out onto the darkness, pure white light shining through. White magic.

It took a while, but eventually, the darkness was half gone. Then, it was more gone than it was there. Soon, I smelled it.

"I smell smoke," I whispered.

Tala laughed. "I feel a breeze!"

Meda poked her head around Phenex to look at us. "Water, Tala. I felt it on my face."

"Keep going," I shouted. We pushed harder, but I began to feel the strain. My body tired with every minute that ticked by. The power ate away at my energy. "We can't stop," I grunted. "Not until every drop of curse is gone."

We kept at it, but when there was barely any blackness left, I felt one of the hands on my back shift.

"I'm having a hard time standing," Gino said faintly.

"I got you," Harper whispered. They shifted behind me, and his hand pressed into me again. "We've got each other," she said. "That's the point."

I wasn't sure if he'd be pulled away from the magical battle if he let go of me, but I didn't want to risk it. "Don't let go!"

Ignoring the tears streaming down my face, I focused on the compassion and acceptance I'd just heard from Harper when speaking to Gino. Using it to bolster my strength, I pushed harder, focusing on the last blob of curse clinging to our combined aura.

It disappeared with a sizzle, and our elements were freed. Air slammed into me. "I can breathe," I said, the tears really flowing now. "I can feel again!" Without removing my arms from around Phenex, I blasted my air out onto the beach, circling our group. Meda and Tala let out strangled yells at the same time I did. I didn't hear what they said over my own excited words, but my air was suddenly filled with fire that warmed and comforted but didn't burn. Rain fell from the sky inside the circle, keeping us from heating too much.

As soon as the three of us had our elements, suddenly the massive, rushing river of power wasn't so unmanageable. I grabbed hold of it like a big blanket, whipping it around.

"It's easy," I breathed.

Meda laughed, unwrapping her arms from around Phenex and pointing at the sky. Fireworks erupted, filling the bright sky with neon sparkles and impossible explosions.

Tala and I let go as well and I realized that with our elements protecting us from the power, we could move independently and direct the power however we needed to.

"Ami," Harper yelled. "Stop!"

I turned to see Gino on the ground in Harper's lap. Noah was shaking him. "He won't wake up," he said, looking up at me.

Inside, he was still with me, his essence clinging to me.

Stop. We have to let the power go. It's hurting our mates.

Meda and Tala froze, looking around. The witches were failing, and the Lycans and vampires looked pale and weak.

On three, direct it into the sky and let go. Close the connection. They nodded at me. *One. Two. Three.*

I slammed my connection to Hell closed and pushed the power still coursing through us up into the sky. Meda grabbed my air and directed it, sending it high to explode in one last massive firework that covered the entire island.

Once the power dissipated, Gino opened his

eyes. I dropped to my knees beside him. "Are you okay?" I asked. "I'm so sorry."

Smiling, he grabbed my hand. "That was so fucking cool."

Everyone laughed. He'd been the most affected, but he'd also not connected to us as much as everyone else. Hopefully, with time, we'd improve our abilities.

"We have enough power to go after Trinity," I said. But, we can't use it until the last minute."

"Agreed," Meda and Tala said in unison.

Meda stood her expression hard. "Let's go fill in the parents. It's time to settle an old score."

CHAPTER EIGHTEEN

After filling our parents in on our development, we had to take a day to finish healing and let our witches recuperate from the toll the massive amount of power had taken on them. In the meantime, we gathered volunteers from the Collective to go with us and mount a strike against Trinity.

The next afternoon, we were finally ready. We stood in the common area of our hotel suite, waiting for the *niswi* to decide who was staying behind with Mom so she wouldn't worry herself into giving birth months too early. Finally, I spoke up. "Because of his connection to Hell, I think Dad should come with us."

The three of them turned their heads in my

direction at the same time. Paw nodded. "I just said that." then he faced Papa. "It's between us."

Papa glanced at all thirteen of us. I could see the desire to go fight in his gaze as well as sense it through our family bond. Paw felt the same, though. They wanted to be with us, help us. "Rock paper scissors?" He held out a fist.

I rolled my eyes and caught Tala and Meda doing the same. Then, we laughed. It was wonderful to be near each other without wanting to claw one another's eyes out. On that thought, I moved closer to them. Meda reached out and grabbed my hand then Tala's. She gave a squeeze. "We're going to win this."

We nodded and several of our mates said, "Hell yeah."

"We're going to kick her ass," Tala said.

Papa cursed, drawing my attention. He lost. At least he got to spend time with Mom alone. Then again, making sure she was relaxed and not pacing their rooms freaking out was a task I didn't wish on anyone.

When Dad and Paw joined us in the center of the common area, Meda nodded to Phenex. "We're ready."

We couldn't go in guns blazing like we'd tried to do when we attempted to rescue Kinsley. The amount of power we could hold now was too hard on our mates. We had to rely on our inherent power and elements until it came time to confront Trinity directly.

Phenex formed the portal to open in the large field outside our dorm at the Collective University. We looked at each other, our mates and *niswi* worried, my sisters and I excited. We knew now that we could handle her. We would be able to save our people. And get revenge on the evil creature that had wreaked havoc on our family since before we were born.

Once everyone was through the portal, Phenex closed it, then the sentries spread out in front of us. My sisters, our mates, and I needed to be fairly close together so we could connect when we pulled all our powers together. I didn't think we'd have to touch to connect this time, but just in case.

I formed an energy ball while adding my air. Damn, it felt good to have all my powers online. Meda and Tala formed their own, only Meda's was more of a high-powered fireball and Tala's was super-charged water ball. I grinned. "On the count of three."

"One," Meda said.

"Two," Tala followed up.

Instead of saying three, the three of us called out to Trinity, snaking power into the air and our voices. Dad had given us a crash-course in demon summoning before we left. With most magic, it was a matter of intent. "Trinity, we summon you."

Like the demon she was.

Within minutes, the air charged with the dark power of Hell. It nipped at my awareness as if saying hello. The air held whispers of the demons who materialized moments later. Figures, the cowardly bitch would send the demons first. But, we'd expected it.

My sisters and I threw our balls of elements and power at the group of demons, then charged at them. Meda conjures swords for Tala and I and then one for herself while pushing her fire to cover the blade. The demons seemed surprised that we had our elements back.

"Yeah, we figured out how to break the curse." I sliced through one demon, then turned, slicing through another. My swords moved in super-speed, now that I had full power and my elements, I was able to use all of my training. I hadn't realized how crippled I'd been by the curse. It had affected more than my elements and mood.

Without it, I was faster, lighter. I caught Harper's

gaze. She grinned at me before jumping straight up in the air, then coming down on top of a demon. She took its head between her hands and jerked, snapping the thing off his shoulders. *Ew. But also yay, Harp!*

Noah and Gino battled a few demons of their own, and I rushed over to them, using their bodies to shield me while formed a large energy ball. Swirling my hands out in front of me, I pulled power from Poppy and Hell. Even though he couldn't be with us in physical form, he was there in spirit—kind of. I felt him briefly as I pulled Hell power into my ball, expanding it with ease. Using the power to create energy balls was far easier and simpler than trying to pull it into myself and direct it, use it.

I tapped into Meda's fire and Tala's water, adding them to the magical cocktail I was forming. Then, my air was last. *Shit, this is huge!*

Meda laughed in my head. *Stop playing with it and throw it already.*

And I did, screaming, "Incoming! Hit the deck!" We'd warned them ahead of time that a huge power-ball was a possibility, and they had to be prepared to drop if they heard us yell.

The sentries, Collective that had volunteered to come help, Dad, Paw, my sisters, and our mates all hit the ground as the large power ball slammed into the crowd of demons. Their screeches echoed around us as they dissolved into black ash.

Everything fell quiet for a few seconds. We looked at each other in amazement. This was how it was supposed to be. We were the most powerful creatures alive. Supposedly ever. Something as mundane as a crowd of demons shouldn't have been so difficult.

Then, the sound of slow clapping made my sisters and I whirl around.

Trinity. Bitch. She walked out of the woods wearing a black, tight-fitted suit. Her white-blond hair looked professionally styled, pulled back in a complicated bun. I saw it when she turned her head to take in the whole group with us. She looked like she belonged on a runway for a Haute-couture business wear designer. If such a brand existed. She was even wearing heels. I tried not to roll my eyes.

"That was very good. Your powers are impressive. But are they enough?" She lifted her hands and we braced ourselves.

Each of us formed energy balls, waiting, no idea what she would do.

Lightning cracked through the sky, then touched down. The ground shook and the shock wave knocked us on our asses. Our hair stood on end as we looked around, our energy balls dissipated.

"What the fuck is that?" Tala yelled, looking at Dad.

"I don't fucking know." Dad's eyes glowed from the power he was pulling from his mother—our Lilipad. "She couldn't do that when I knew her." Then he threw his energy ball at Trinity. The demonic bitch deflected it like it was nothing more than a gnat.

"What happened to you, Trin?" he called.

She cocked her head at him. "How would you respond to the death of your child?"

"Before that. We were best friends. Why'd you have to ruin everything?"

She smiled and sucked in a deep breath. Trinity was calling on the electricity in the atmosphere again. We had to pull all our powers together. All thirteen of us, and we had to do it quick. Problem was, we'd only ever done it once. There was no time to practice it over and over.

"Meda. Tala."

Meda nodded, knowing what I was thinking. It was great to be connected again. I'd missed my sisters in my head. "Dad. Paw. Get the sentries to distract her long enough for us all to connect."

"On it," Paw said.

Dad strode forward. "Stop this, Trinity. You had such a promising future. You can't win this."

She laughed maniacally and engaged him in conversation. I heard her daughter's name but ignored her words as we focused on connecting.

Our mates closed in. I met Meda's gaze. "I think if we all hold hands we'd have enough contact to connect."

"I think so too." She grabbed Peter's and then Sterling's hand. Dorian took Sterling's, then held his out to Kevin. We formed a circle with our backs facing inside so we weren't vulnerable to whatever Trinity threw at us. She would try to take advantage of any weakness she saw.

Phenex joined the circle last, standing in the center, not touching us, but I felt him inside me. Apparently, being connected to all of us when we broke the curse was good enough to link him to all our mates. Good to know. He was truly our center now.

I opened the link to Hell and pulled in my sisters. This time it went fast, which was great since Trinity had turned her attention back to us.

Each of them pulled in their mates. We didn't bother doing it one at a time because we didn't have time. I heard a few curses from our mates but they didn't pull away. It must've been uncomfortable, being sucked in quickly.

"Ready?" Meda asked as Trinity raised her arms. "It's going to be hard and fast."

"That's what she said," Kevin said. Then he grunted when Tala elbowed him in the ribs. "Sorry."

Holding in my giggle because it was funny, and because I was freaking stressed out, I counted down. "Together on three."

"One," Meda whispered as a bolt of lightning streaked across the sky. It was taking Trinity longer to call it down this time.

"Two," Tala followed up.

Again, instead of saying three, we pulled on the power of Hell and threw our magic and elements into the link at the same time. Phenex served as a central power source, and I hadn't realized just how much he had held back from us until that moment. Even on the beach, he hadn't given us his full ability. Glancing over my shoulder I saw him lift his arms, and a large ball of power, fire, water, and air formed over us. It contained power from each of us and hell.

When it was larger than our circle, he threw it right at Trinity and the new group of demons that had run out of the trees to join her. It killed all the demons as soon as it touched them but didn't touch Trinity.

"Fuck," several of our mates said at once.

"How the hell is she still standing?" Tala growled.

That didn't make sense. "Who is she connected to that can give her that much power?" She had to be linked to someone powerful in Hell. It was the only thing that would give her that much power. "What now?"

Meda growled then looked at me. "Can you freeze her?"

"I think so. I should be able to." I focused on Trinity and called to my time manipulation power. Usually, I just needed to focus on something and simply will it to freeze. It didn't need to be spoken out loud. However, it wasn't affecting Trinity. "It's not working."

We'd waited too long. Trinity's lightning returned, blasting inside our circle. We were ripped apart and thrown in all directions. I climbed to my feet, blood running down my forehead and into my eye. As I tried to wipe it away, I looked around to see Gino lying unconscious on the ground.

"No," I whispered, but I couldn't hear my voice. The blast had messed with my ears. Rushing to my mate, I was relieved to find him stirring. The blast had knocked him out, but he was rallying.

Tala and Meda had their mates around them again, and Phenex sat beside them, holding his head. He'd probably been closest to the bolt when it hit the ground.

I grabbed Gino with Harper's help and hobbled over to my family.

To buy us time, Dad had attacked Trinity hand-to-hand, but she was playing with him. She was faster than any vampire had ever been, darting around him with maniacal laughter pouring out of her mouth.

"Connect again," Tala said. "I have an idea."

We drew together. I didn't know whose hand I grabbed, but soon we huddled close, everyone touching more than one person. I opened up the flow of power, and as soon as it touched me, my ears cleared, and I could hear again.

Tala got quiet, her total focus was on Trinity. The demonic vamp jerked her gaze to Tala as if the two of them had connected in some way. Calmly, and with a cold tone, Tala said, "Form another power ball, bigger than the last one and when I say the word, Ami, freeze her." She narrowed her gaze on Trinity, tears pouring down her cheeks. As I pulled on her power to form the ball, I gasped. Her emotions were consumed with grief.

Okay. I didn't ask questions. Whatever she was doing, she thought it would work. I kept funneling power into the ball.

I felt Phenex behind us, pulling on more power, and I pushed my air to him, knowing that Meda and Tala added their elements. I also felt our witches adding their magic in the mix. This had to work.

Trinity snarled and walked toward us. Tala laughed, but the sound was evil, sending a shiver up my spine. I'd heard her be mean, careless, thoughtless. This, though, was a cruel joy. It struck me deep inside. Tala had power none of us understood yet.

Suddenly, Trinity stopped her stalk and gasped, clutching her chest, sobbing as tears rolled down her face.

Tala said, "Now Ami." Tala's voice was choked, full of pain. I looked at her as I pulled on my power. Her red face was tortured, liquid running out of her eyes and nose as she focused on Trinity.

"Freeze," I commanded. I didn't want to freeze time, just her. I'd never tried it before, but with the massive amount of power flowing through me, I willed it to be so.

Trinity froze.

Without breaking our link, Meda stepped forward. "This is how your daughter died, bitch."

Then Meda took control over the energy ball and used my air to control it. The ball shrank as it neared Trinity, but the power stayed inside. Condensed. Trinity's eyes followed the power as it floated in the air toward her. As the ball reached Trinity's forehead, it was the size of a marble but had enough power in it to level a small city. I stepped forward and took Meda's hand again. Tala did the same. We focused, and the power ball burrowed into Trinity's head as she screamed.

The sound would haunt me for years to come. The sound of an animal dying a painful, horrific. death. It was well-deserved, but the shriek chilled me to the bone.

The scream didn't stop until Trinity burst into black ash.

I stared at Meda as a calm settled around us. "Damn, Meda, that was dark."

Meda shrugged, unconcerned. "I'm the granddaughter of Lucifer. I'm a little dark."

CHAPTER NINETEEN

*J*released the power of Hell abruptly, sinking to the ground. "It's over," I whispered. "She's dead." Running through the psychic connection I had to my mates, sisters, and parents, I made sure they were all alive. Their links pulsed with various levels of pain, grief, and worry, but everyone was still there.

Focusing my depleted energy, I plucked at the threads between worlds, opening a small portal into Mom's bedroom. "Hey," I called to her back. She whirled around. "Ami!" Rushing forward, she tried to look through the opening, but I'd only made it big enough for my face. "None of the family died, but I have no idea the injuries or deaths of anyone else yet. I'm lagging but wanted you to know. Trinity is dead."

The edges of a portal burned too much to touch, so she pressed a kiss to the tips of her index and middle finger and then pressed her fingers to my lips. "All my love, bring everyone home safe to me."

I let go of the threads of the portal and collapsed, letting my head settle onto the soft grass. I hadn't been directly injured, but I felt more burned through now than I had the day before when we'd handled the power together for the first time.

Rolling onto my side, I looked at the scene. My sisters and all our mates were the only ones lying on the ground in exhaustion. Everyone else milled around, checking injuries and helping others to their feet. Paw and Dad walked around the wounded, looking for the worst injuries.

My sisters laid behind me, and our mates were trying to get to their feet. No doubt they wanted to get to us.

I smiled to see Harper sit down beside Gino and draw his head into her lap. She spoke to him and touched his face. It wasn't sexual or even loving. She was caring for him. I felt for her in my mind, and concern flowed. She looked up at me when she felt me checking on her. I shot her a weary smile that she returned.

Noah got to his feet and stumbled over. "You

okay?" he whispered. He knew I was, but he wanted to be near me as much as I wanted to be near him, Harper, and Gino.

"Yeah. I will be. If you can, will you help check on the wounded?"

He nodded. "I'm not hurt, just worn out."

"I think that's all of us," I said.

"My mates are okay," Tala said behind me. "Meda?"

Meda nodded, dragging herself into a sitting position. "Yeah."

Slowly, the wounded were gathered, and the dead carried inside the dorm building to wait for their families.

We'd only lost two, but it was two too many. Sentries, they'd lost their lives making sure nothing could get to us while we took care of Trinity.

They'd be honored.

Phenex had a bit more stamina than the rest of us, having manipulated power for many, many years longer than we had. He gathered the wounded and opened a portal. "I'll send them to the infirmary," he told my Dad.

"We had an infirmary on the island?" I asked. I'd managed to get to my feet and walk over to Phenex.

My sisters were still working on it. "We might need to see the Shaman," I told Phenex.

He put his hand on my forehead and closed his eyes. "I'll check your sisters out, too, but I think it's just burn out."

"Burn out?" My sisters walked up as I spoke.

"Is that why I feel like the end of a blown-out match?" Meda asked.

Phenex nodded. "You'll recover, but it'll take a few days. Your witches look like they'll need the most care."

I turned to find Harper and Noah holding Gino up. "Can we go home, or back to the island, or wherever it is we're going?" Harp asked. "We can't hold him up for long."

Phenex nodded. "I think it would be easiest to return to the island for the night and give everyone the option of going home or staying."

Dad sucked in a deep breath. "Yes, I agree."

Phenex opened a portal and ushered the wounded through. "I'll help the shaman if you can get everyone else back," he said.

I nodded. "I think I can handle enough to make a portal," I said.

It wasn't easy, as it turned out, but I managed to make three. One at the entrance to each of the hotels on Poppy's island, allowing the Collective members that had volunteered to fight to exit at the point closest to their families.

Many hugs and congratulations were given. It was hard to smile and accept the compliments when two more dead bodies lay a few feet away inside the dorm building.

My parents would have to deliver the news to two more sets of families. Families that were, at this moment, waiting for news of their relatives.

Finally, everyone was through except my sisters, their mates, Paw, and Dad. I created one last portal, then followed everyone through, closing it with a snap, then collapsing on the couch.

"Someone else is going to have to move our mattresses so we can have a puppy pile," I said wearily. "I can't do it."

"We can," Dad said. "We're tired, but nothing like you lot."

Our wonderful *niswi* moved the couch with me, Meda, and Tala lying on it, curled around each other in a tangle of limbs.

"Tala," I said, raising my head. "What did you do to her?"

"Trinity?" she asked.

I nodded my head, but I had no idea if she saw me.

She must have because she continued. "I have no clue what made it pop into my head. Or why I've never thought of it before. But, her grief was pressing at the wall I keep to hold off my emotions." I knew what she was talking about. Poppy had helped her create it years ago, and it kept her empath abilities from overwhelming her. It also made her a callous bitch sometimes. But, we loved her anyway.

"I opened myself to it. Absorbed it. It was significant. She carried around a lot of pain." Tala shuddered. "Something inside me told me I could give it back to her. So, I tried. And I amplified it. I grabbed the fear and pain of the people around me and stuffed it into her grief—somehow."

"And when you gave it back to her, it overwhelmed her?" Randell asked. I looked up to see everyone in the room was staring at Tala with their jaws slack.

"Damn, Talls," Peter said. "You're scary AF."

"I keep trying to tell you that, but nobody believes me," Tala grumbled.

We chuckled, everyone too weary and sad to muster a real laugh.

Soon, the *niswi* had our mattresses laid out. We

climbed into bed, knees over legs, arms over stomachs. I was pretty sure my feet were tucked halfway under Randell, and Meda's butt was crammed into my back. Phenex walked in as we started to drift off and wiggled into the middle of us all, sighing in relief. "I can't believe how happy I am to be here," he said. "A few weeks ago, I would've laughed at anyone that said I'd be here now."

"Go to sleep, Phenex," Tala said.

"Yes, Tala," he replied.

"Goodnight girls," my mother's voice drifted over us. "Goodnight, uh, everyone else."

Soft laughter filled the air as those of us still awake chuckled at my mother's awkward show of affection for our ridiculous number of mates.

It was over. Maybe now life could go back to normal.

Whatever normal was.

EPILOGUE

POPPY

My girls had no idea I watched them. They had no idea of a lot of things. For now. I'd need them soon, but they had a few years before I had to disrupt their lives.

They'd defeated Trinity beautifully. I'd watched that as well, jumping for joy in my bedroom as I watched through a carefully placed portal.

Meda had kicked major ass. "I'm the granddaughter of Lucifer," she'd said. I chuckled remembering her sass.

All three of them had shown their extreme strength. Tala, using her empathy at the last minute was a stroke of genius. I probably should've taught her how to do that years ago. Oh, well, better to learn things by doing. She'd never forget it now.

My girls sat in the huge library of the home Meda's mate had bought them, blankets spread around and a roaring fire in the mantel. They'd figured out they were much stronger together and had been spending a lot of time together since they killed Trinity.

"What are you doing?" my Lilith asked, walking into my room. I indicated the window to the Earth realm, so she could see her girls.

"Oh, they look so tired," she said.

"They're exhausted. But Trinity is gone, and they have time to rest."

Lilith sucked in a breath. "What have you Seen?"

I hated to tell her. "Lilith, time passes differently on Earth, you know that. When we close this window and go to bed, we'll wake up tomorrow to find months or years have passed there."

She nodded. "Yes, but we always make it work." Furrowing her brow, she put a hand on my arm. To us, she'd only been with me in Hell for almost a year. On Earth, it had been more than eighteen. I hated to break the news to her. "Lucifer, what is it?"

She'd been distant since I forced her to return. But I'd *Seen* what was coming, knew it would take everything I had, every bit of support at my disposal.

The day my son was born, I *Saw* the future of my family. My heirs.

Lilith didn't want to be here, but I'd had no other choice. She was the wife of my choice. No other woman had ever made me a fraction as happy as Lilith. I hadn't even looked sideways at another woman since Kane was born. Watching her birth my son had cemented my love for her in my heart. Having her here with me when he was an infant had been the happiest time of my life. Then she'd left, to raise him on Earth. I'd told her he would one day rule the vampires. It was important he be in the right places at the right times, to meet his mate.

Unfortunately, my beautiful lover didn't return my affection. She viewed me as a good time in bed, and I gave her the power she loved. I almost chuckled. That woman loved wearing a crown.

I hated to make her face fall into worry, but there was no choice. "The contracts are gone," I said. "All of them."

"What do you mean, *gone?*" She stepped back, looking through the window at our granddaughters and their mates. Mates I'd carefully selected years ago, appealing to the ancestors. Nobody knew I had power there.

I had power everywhere. Everywhere except Heaven.

Nobody knew I'd made sure, from the moment my son was born, that events would lead to this day.

If I hadn't, there would never be enough power to defeat him.

I put my hands on Lilith's arms. "Sammael has returned."

Thank you so much for taking this journey with Media, Tala, and Ami. It's been one hell of a ride.

So what's next in the collective world?
Poppy and Lilipad, of course!

The first book in the Lucifer's War Trilogy, Consort, is available for preorder and releases January 22, 2020!
Click Here to Preorder your copy

Dead Air is a steamy Reverse Harem paranormal romance novel set in the **Collective World**. Please see the suggested reading order for the **Collective World** below.

Please note, **Academy's Rise** -- *Hell Fire, Dark Waters, Dead Air* -- can be read as a stand-alone trilogy. The below reading order is only suggested.

Welcome to the *Collective World*

Coven's End

Kane

Voss

Quin

Jillian

The Complete Series Bundle

Academy's Rise

Hell Fire

Dark Water

Dead Air

Lucifer's War

Consort

Assassin

Queen

ABOUT LIA DAVIS

Lia Davis is the USA Today bestselling author of more than forty books, including her fan favorite Ashwood Falls Series.

A lifelong fan of magic, mystery, romance and adventure, Lia's novels feature compassionate alpha heroes and strong leading ladies, plenty of heat, and happily-ever-afters.

Lia makes her home in Northeast Florida where she battles hurricanes and humidity like one of her heroines.

When she's not writing, she loves to spend time with her family, travel, read, enjoy nature, and spoil her kitties.

She also loves to hear from her readers. Send her a note at lia@authorliadavis.com!

Follow Lia on Social Media

Website: http://www.authorliadavis.com/

Newsletter: http://www.subscribepage.com/authorliadavis.newsletter

Facebook author fan page: https://www.facebook.com/novelsbylia/

Facebook Fan Club: https://www.facebook.com/groups/LiaDavisFanClub/

Twitter: https://twitter.com/novelsbylia

Instagram: https://www.instagram.com/authorliadavis/

BookBub: https://www.bookbub.com/authors/lia-davis

Pinterest: http://www.pinterest.com/liadavis35/

Goodreads: http://www.goodreads.com/author/show/5829989.Lia_Davis

His Big Bad Wolf (MM)

Their Royal Ash

Tempting the Wolf

Hexed with Sass (part of the Milly Taiden Sassy Ever After World)

Claiming Her Dragons (Part of the Milly Taiden Paranormal Dating Agency)

Contemporaries

Pleasures of the Heart Series

Single Titles

His Guarded Heart (MM)

ABOUT LAINIE ANDERSON

Lainie lives in East Tennessee with her husband, three children, and an ever growing number of cats. She loves reading, watching TV, and procrastinating by browsing Facebook. Lainie's passions include vampires, food, and listening to heavy metal music. She once won a Harry Potter trivia contest based on the books and lost one based on the movies. She has two bands on her bucket list that she still hasn't seen: AC/DC and Alice Cooper. Feel free to send tickets.

Dark Water

Dead Air

Lucifer's War (Paranormal Romance)

COMPLETE SERIES

Devil's Consort

Devil's Assassin

Valentine Pride (Paranormal Reverse Harem)

COMPLETE SERIES

Series Boxed Set

Unicorn Mates

Unicorn Luck

http://www.books2read.com/Leola3

A Platypus and Her Mates

Magic & Metaphysics Academy (Paranormal
Academy Reverse Harem)

COMPLETE SERIES

Series Boxed Set

Magical Mischief

Magical Mistake

Magical Misfit

Southern Soil (Sweet Contemporary Reverse Harem):

Literary Yours

Snow Cure